The Vergrinn War

Book One

The Risen Spear

By Scott Biddle

Lydia,

Keep hustling and keep smiling!

Coach Aust

Table of Contents

Prologue

As the moon rose over the horizon, Whitefoot looked out over the clench. Thousands were already here, and thousands more were streaming in from outlying villages and more remote tribal grounds. The Great Cull was more than 600 moons in the past and he was the only warrior who had returned from it. This clench wasn't quite as large as the last clench before the Cull, but it might be close. As he watched the clench form, his mind wandered back to the way events had unfolded over time to bring them here.

The Cull had cost him many friends and clanmates as well as an eye and an ear, and if he had followed Pack tradition of fighting to the death it would have cost him his life and might have been the end of the Pack as he knew it. When the Cull happened, however, Whitefoot had been sent back by his sire with a message to the rest of the Pack to go into hiding lest their enemies seek out the old, the young, and the nursing mothers who had been left behind. Their enemies often called it "withdrawing" or "retreating" and his sire had explicitly ordered his withdrawal, but deep in his heart he had felt that he was betraying his friends, his family, and himself as he watched his brothers and sisters and sire being slain and the heaps of Pack dead rising higher and higher.

Upon his return the remaining Pack members had been silent, but they had obeyed. Whitefoot's sire had, after all, been the Alpha and it was widely expected that one of his pups would someday take his place. The Pack had withdrawn to the barren hills of the far north. The hunting wasn't as good, but there weren't as many mouths to feed and there were many caves in which to hide while the Pack grew strong again.

After a hundred moons had passed and a new generation of warriors was almost ready, the Pack had begun to expand their territory. They stayed to the north and stayed near the barren lands, but the harsh environment made the young warriors stronger. After two hundred more moons had passed, the Pack started to gradually encroach upon the woodlands near the barrens.

Another hundred moons of gradual expansion brought them near their old territory, but also brought terrifying news – the old enemy had been sighted! They were in tiny villages near the Pack's old hunting grounds and only a few had been seen, but they were there. Whitefoot had sent scouts throughout the land, and for the next hundred moons they were silent observers. They brought the news that as far as the great neck between the lands there were villages of the enemy, and that near the site of the Great Cull they had set a mighty walled village in the heart of the Pack's hunting grounds.

For the last hundred moons, Whitefoot had been coming up with devices to reclaim the Pack's territory and eventually wipe out all remnants of the enemy, so that hundreds of moons after he had passed they would not arise and wipe out the Pack as he intended to do to them now. He had doubled the number of scouts (which occasionally meant that one was observed – then being forced to kill and consume his observer to avoid detection) and he had started some of his most intelligent and dexterous folk to constructing tools such as he had seen among the enemy.

As the moon reached its zenith, the crowd had finished assembling and grew eerily quiet as they waited for Whitefoot to address them. He looked out over three generations of warriors who would be departing soon. "My children, tonight is a night long awaited. Too long have we lain hidden in fear. Tonight we set out to reclaim our birthright and destroy our enemy and avenge our ancestors. We will drink their blood and feast upon the tender flesh of their young before the next moon rises. Tonight the Pack sets out on The Great Hunt. The First Claw is already on their way to prepare the way for us and now we set forth to join them. To the hunt!" A great howl arose over the valley as the Pack departed.

Chapter One

Amundr was excited. Today was Market day, and that meant that he and his father would soon be heading into town to trade. He was sitting at the table eating eggs and sausage while his father reminded him of his responsibilities. "Remember, you need to load all of those skins and all of the meat that is finished curing into the wagon. I'll see to the team and gather our provisions for tonight and tomorrow."

"Yes, father."

"And if we do well at Market today, I will get something for you. You have certainly earned it."

"Thank you, father!" THAT was a surprise. Amundr's father Olafr loved him dearly and he knew it, but he had always been a frugal man. Amundr's mind raced – what would his father think of as doing "well" and what would his gift be? There were so many amazing things at Market, colorful clothing and useful tools and weapons and animals and unusual foods. Amundr couldn't wait to see what the surprise was.

Amundr raced out to the shed to start gathering things for the trip to Market and was nearly bowled over by Samr and Gramr, the elkhounds that were somewhat his. The truth was that these dogs had happened by the house a few winters ago and Amundr started feeding them some of the scraps from the table. After they had been around for a year, Olafr had come to trust them enough that he would let Amundr spend a whole day hunting in the woods alone with them. They were large – almost as large as a wolf. With the two of them along Amundr didn't fear any creatures he might meet save the largest bears, and his father took the bears near them before they grew that large. Unfortunately, the large and occasionally playful dogs were too much trouble to take to Market, so they were always left at the house while Amundr and Olafr went to town.

Their wares and provisions soon loaded onto their wagon, the team of draft horses was hitched up and father and son set out for Market. Amundr's mind wandered back to the promise of a gift and the journey to the town of Eyjolf flew by.

***

Amundr was bored. Market day was usually exciting, but it was almost midday and his best friend Saegrimr hadn't arrived. Amundr and Saegrimr had both seen fifteen winters, but Saegrimr was born in the spring and thought that being six months older made him wiser and smarter than Amundr. Saegrimr took advantage of their age difference to kiddingly refer to his friend as "little Mundi," just like Amundr's father used to when he was a child.

Every Sjaundi the town of Eyjolf held Market, and Amundr had been coming in with his father to sell skins, antlers, and meat for as long as he could remember. They lived about a league northwest of Eyjolf in a small cottage near a densely wooded area, and they spent most of their days in the woods nearby, hunting and trapping bear and elk and moose for meat and hides to trade in town. They had a modest garden in a clearing near their cottage (the lumber for their cottage had been hewn from those trees) and Amundr's mother had taught him how to tend the garden when he was too young to accompany his father into the woods. His mother had died seven winters ago bearing Amundr's younger brother, who had followed her the next day, and since that winter Amundr and his father had lived alone.

Each spring they would fix up damage caused to the cottage by the harsh winters and they would tend their garden. They didn't hunt much at that time because his father explained that this was the time when animals were growing large enough to be eaten as well as bearing and tending new offspring which could be hunted in future years. In summer they plied the river in their boat and fished, trapping small game for meat and fur. They would harvest the spices and vegetables that had grown in their garden and lay in stores for the coming winter. In the fall they would hunt and kill many fat creatures and salt and smoke most of the meat. They would tan the hides and gather the furs, and the market days in the fall were the best of all. Today was one such day – they had a dozen bear skins, many elk hides and lots of smoked meat to trade along with a few smaller hides, teeth, claws, and antlers from a variety of creatures. His father was the best hunter for miles around and occasionally the baron's own hunting guide, Stigr, would come seeking his advice.

The trading had apparently gone better than he could have hoped, because a few minutes ago his father had presented him with a new knife and fifteen steel arrowheads of his own. His father had taught him how to make flint arrowheads, but the steel ones stayed sharper longer and didn't break as easily.

"You've earned it. Three of those bears were your kills along with two of the elk. If you hadn't had to spend so much time making new points for your arrows we'd have had even more to trade today." What his father didn't tell him was that he had been saving up for a while to purchase these and he had also purchased a much finer spear for both Amundr and himself that he intended to give him at Yule.

Amundr wandered around the various stalls, chewing on some dried bear meat he had brought and drinking in the sundry smells and looking at the varied wares. He really hoped Saegrimr arrived soon, because his family raised sheep and produced some of the finest mutton around. As well as this day was going for his father he imagined that they might roast a lamb over the fire tonight. They usually camped just outside the city walls with most of the other outlying folk who came to town for Market day and stayed for Worship the next day. Saegrimr's family usually camped as close to Amundr and his father as possible and they would share their meals together that night.

After the midday meal, Amundr was playing with some puppies at one of the stalls. They were elkhounds, and reminded him of Samr and Gramr. He gave each of them a small strip of bear meat and headed over to look at some chickens. People started to murmur around him and he noticed that there was some commotion off to the northwest. There were half a dozen people approaching fast on horseback and in the distance they could see a small train of wagons.

As the riders neared, Amundr saw that one of them was Saegrimr's father, Holmr, and that all the horses and riders were bloody, and several of them had large sacks across their horses' backs that appeared to have been soaked through with blood. As they approached the city gate, Holmr shouted

"Where's the Baron? Summon the muster. The vergrinn are coming!"

Chapter Two

Vergrinn! Amundr thought they were simply a tale told by the fires to scare the children. Vergrinn were wolves who walked upright and spoke in a strange tongue and ate people. Surely he must not have heard that correctly.

Horns were sounding and people were running to the gate as fast as they could. The word was spreading like wildfire through the Market and the rest of the town. Holmr and the men with him rode up the street to the keep, where they dismounted and were led inside. The people around burst into motion as parents sought out children and children sought out parents. As Amundr turned from the gate to find his father he heard his name being called from an approaching wagon.

"Amundr! Little Mundi! Over here!"

Saegrimr was here and he was alive. Amundr ran out towards the wagon that was just now coming to a stop. Surely his friend would be able to tell him what was happening. "Did you really see the vergrinn?!"

His friend shook his head, "I didn't actually see any, but we could all hear them in the distance. My father and several of the other men saw them and brought back a few heads and paws to show people that they really are vergrinn, but as soon as we knew what was happening they gathered all of us onto wagons and sent us towards Eyjolf so that we could get into the city and find protection. Father and the others rode out to warn people living outside of our village which is why they only got here just ahead of us even though the wagons were so much slower."

"Where did they come from? How many are there? What do they want?" Amundr was frantic, but his friend merely shook his head.

***

Inside the keep Holmr and the baron were having a similar conversation. "Do you have any idea how many there are?" the baron asked.

"We went back to look around and it was obvious that there were hundreds, maybe thousands." Holmr was an elder in his small village as well as an experienced fighter, having led his village's defense against various raiding parties and brigands over the years and understood the importance of finding out such information. "We sent half a dozen men on the fastest steeds we had to try to find out. Hopefully they will let us know soon."

"How did we find them, or should I ask how they found us?" the baron asked.

"As far as we can tell, they had a small advanced scouting party out ahead of their main force. Five of them apparently came across a hunter near our village and attacked him. He fled towards the village and they pursued. We killed four of the five but it cost us a dozen men plus the hunter who died of his wounds. The fifth devil fled to the north and we tracked him for a couple of hours before we heard the sounds of more in the distance and decided that we needed to seek the shelter of the city. We've gathered in all of the people between our village and here."

At that moment they were interrupted by one of the door wardens, "Milord, we have riders here that wish to speak to both of you."

"Show them in."

Three riders came in, clearly winded and looking alarmed. The first spoke immediately "Milord, the news is grim. We went east to the river and then turned north to observe from Eagle Point. There are at least two thousands of the devils camped two leagues northeast of our village. We could also see that apparently the other three men who went out with us but turned west got too close to the devils and they and their horses were treating the vergrinn to a midday feast," he shuddered as he spoke. "What's more, some of the vergrinn carried axes and some of the trees around them were felled as we watched. I don't know what they are up to, but it can't be good."

The baron was uncertain. "How can we be certain these are vergrinn? The vergrinn were wiped out fifty years ago and no one has seen them since. I've never heard of one retreating as you described, and they've never before shown the subtlety to scout or move cautiously. They've never used a tool before, either."

Holmr shook his head. "I've never heard of anything like this in the old stories either, but as for the question of whether they are vergrinn..." He nodded to one of the men who had come in with him and that man dumped the contents of the bag he was carrying onto the cold stone floor. The overly large wolf head with its relatively small snout rolled to a stop near the baron's feet with the eyes staring blankly up at him. "It walked on two feet and used a spear. They're currently eating the remains of some of my men and their horses. If that's not a vergrinn, it might as well be."

The baron was stunned into silent thought. This town had been built and this barony had been established under his father as an outpost against the vergrinn after their defeat at the Battle of the Glade fifty years ago. The Glade was only a league and a half from here and they still used the tales to frighten children. He came to a decision. "Warn all the guards on the walls to redouble their watch, and summon everyone else to the church."

***

There was anxious murmuring making its way through the crowd in the church building as they waited for the baron to arrive and start speaking. Everyone there had heard the rumor about the vergrinn and they all wanted to know what they were going to do. In theory, the church building was big enough for everyone to meet together to worship but the truth was that with everyone in there it was a tight fit and there were people gathered outside near the windows and door.

Finally the baron made his way to the front of the building with the city elders and the crowd quieted down. One of the city elders stepped forward to word a prayer, "Oh great and wonderful God, provider of all that is good. We thank you for the bountiful harvest you have provided us this year and for the many daily blessings we receive from you. We humbly beseech you now for your guidance and protection in this time of trial and we pray that our faith in you remains strong."

The elder stepped back and the baron stepped forward. "By now I am certain that all of you have heard. The vergrinn have returned. Their numbers are great and they are behaving strangely. Right now

I am telling you that we will bring all food goods into the keep and we will ration provisions as if we were under siege." There was some grumbling at this, but most of the older citizens nodded in approval.

"Furthermore, we do not know if we will be able to hold the town. We may have to retreat into the keep if we are overwhelmed, and the keep is not large enough for everyone to stay in there." This caused the grumbling to increase in volume. "I have discussed it with the city elders and we have decided on a course of action. All children who have less than sixteen winters and their mothers will be loaded onto wagons and sent south to the Duke's citadel in Gudmund."

A man in the front row exclaimed "They'll be eaten for sure! You're sending our women and children to their deaths to save yourself!"

The baron shook his head. "My own son Aoalbert will be with the wagons, and I will send a dozen men with the wagons for their protection. They will likely be safer than we who remain here. Furthermore, there are several lads of fourteen or fifteen winters who would have been joining the muster soon. These lads will be added to the muster early and will provide additional protection." Amundr turned and saw that Saegrimr's surprise was clearly as great as his own. They were both supposed to join the muster this summer and they both knew how to use a spear and a bow, but the sudden weight of helping guard a caravan of women and children as they fled to the safety of the regional capital nearly overwhelmed Amundr.

The baron named the men who were to guide and guard the caravan, and they included two of his household knights known for their horsemanship and prowess in battle, two merchants who were most familiar with the road to the capital, the two best woodsmen in the barony – his own hunting guide Stigr and Amundr's father, and half a dozen other men of the muster. He informed them that the wagons were already being prepared and provisioned and that they thought it would take them a week to get to the city and that hopefully in another week the Duke's men would be riding to relieve the city. They would depart in two hours so that they could be as far away as possible by tomorrow when the vergrinn came to town.

***

As the crowd went their ways to gather supplies into the keep and make other preparations, Amundr's father pulled him aside and steered him towards their wagon. "Little Mundi, today you are being given a man's responsibility. I know you are more ready for this than any of the boys your age, and my heart swells with pride when I think of this. I have something for you." He reached for the new spear he had bought for him and handed it over. "Amundr, remember that the spear is not as

XX

important as the hand that wields it, and the hand is not as important as the heart that moves it – but a sharp spear is always better than a dull one in either case."

Amundr and his father headed for the barracks near the gate where the men who were escorting the wagons were assembling. None of the other young men's fathers were going along on the journey and all of them were outside in the courtyard getting some hurried instruction in the proper use of their spears and shields, but Amundr walked alongside his father into the barracks – he had killed bears and wolves with his spear and wanted to be treated like one of the men. He received some odd looks from some of the men assembled, and the Baron looked at him long and hard for what felt like an hour but couldn't have been more than a few seconds. Finally the Baron withdrew his gaze and spoke.

"This will not be easy. Every one of you will be sorely missed from our ramparts, but all of you also realize that the desperate straits we are in will likely be the death of those that remain behind. For those of us remaining behind our hope is that we can hold out for a time and inflict significant losses on our foe and keep their attention from following you. Your duty is twofold – you must protect the women and children who depart with you and you must warn the Duke of the dangers of the vergrinn. My son goes with you, and while I know that every man in this room possesses more skill on the field of battle and in the woodlands..." and with that he looked at Amundr, "My son must grow into his role as the next Baron of Eyjolf. He is by birthright a knight of Eyjolf and by law the highest ranking man among you. He has, unfortunately, been ill prepared for this moment by a father who spoiled him while growing complacent and who convinced himself that the threat we were appointed to watch for was gone forever. I ask for three things – your oath to serve him as you would me and to fulfill the mission given to you, your assistance in guiding him towards the right choices, and your forgiveness for being saddled with this." He lowered his eyes as he said the last. Every man in the room stepped forward and kneeled before the baron, including Amundr, and swore their lives to his house and to the mission before them.

As they all rose to leave, the baron called Olafr and Amundr aside. "Olafr, you are the most skilled man on this mission and by rights you should be the leader. All of the men know this and they will all follow your lead in whatever you do. Please watch out for my son." Olafr nodded and walked away.

Chapter Three

It was still a few hours before sunset when the caravan set out. Each wagon carried more than a dozen women and children with light provisions for a week and the total number on the wagons exceeded seven score. The knights and the men of the muster rode sturdy horses, including Saegrimr and Aoalbert, who rode their own steeds. Amundr rode a spirited chestnut stallion. His father had traded his team and wagon for a sturdy riding horse for himself and his son. The rest of the newest young members of the muster rode in the wagons with their mothers and brothers and sisters and everyone silently prayed that they could ride there in peace. Following the advice of Olafr they set out due south along the road at the best speed they could make. Their plan was to make for a small hill four leagues south of town to camp for the night.

As the sun was dropping behind the trees, the caravan of wagons turned west off the road up a little used path and the wagons trundled up a low hill. The underbrush was relatively thick and the branches grabbed at horse and rider as they ascended. It was clear that no wagons had passed this way in quite some time. As they neared the top of the hill Olafr called a halt and silently dropped from his saddle to examine the ground. He called several of the other men over and they held a whispered conversation.

Into the middle of this conversation rode Aoalbert. "What's the holdup?" he demanded. "We're almost to the top of the hill and all of you just stopped. Our horses are tired and the people are tired. Move along and let us continue!"

The men gathered around Olafr hesitated and looked to Olafr. "Sir, I beg your pardon but we were examining tracks on the ground." He began. "The tracks were rather unusual and looked quite like they might have been made by vergrinn several days ago."

"Vergrinn tracks? Here? Preposterous. All of you heard just as I did that they are coming from the north, not the south. Besides, if they were coming from the south we would have passed them as we traveled."

"Well, sir..." Olafr hesitated "It seems as though the vergrinn may be ahead of us as well. We know they have sent out small groups to scout ahead, and it may be that they have sent additional scouts past Eyjolf and possibly as far as the isthmus of Gudmund. We may want to reconsider our path and take a longer route to avoid the road."

"If we take a longer path then we might run out of food. If we take a longer path then we might not reach Gudmund in time to send back help to Eyjolf. If we take a longer path then I will have to put up with the incessant whining and the stench of these peasants for longer than necessary!" Aoalbert was practically screaming by the time he finished his rant. Amundr personally thought that the first two points were valid, but thought that Aoalbert had whined as much as any newborn on the first part of their journey.

Olafr came close to Aoalbert so no others would hear and said "If we take the shorter path and run into vergrinn, we won't need to worry about food. We also won't need to worry about sending folks back to help and we will long for the cries of babies instead of the howls of vergrinn, milord."

That brought Aoalbert up short and he quickly dismounted. "Show me the tracks."

"Unfortunately, milord, in your haste you rode through them and they are mostly trampled. You can still make out this one over here and that one over there," Olafr pointed with the butt of his spear, "But there are not enough left for us to determine how many vergrinn there were or how long ago they were here."

"How can you tell those are vergrinn tracks? They look similar to wolf tracks." Amundr was shocked to learn that the baron's son actually knew what a wolf's tracks looked like.

"Well, the feet are longer and the spacing between the pads on the paws is different on a vergrinn. Also, when there were more tracks we could look at the spacing between the tracks from when they stood still and when they walked. These creatures were only walking on one pair of feet."

"Well, let's continue with caution to the top of the hill and we'll decide in the morning which path to take from here."

"Yes, milord."

***

The horses and wagons reached the top of the hill without further incident, but as they were not building fires or setting up tents, there was little to do to set up their camp. Olafr sent men out in pairs to scout around the hill – a veteran paired with a newly minted "warrior" – and they all reported back that they had not seen anything unusual. A small group was sent down to a nearby stream to fetch water and haul it back to the camp and then everyone settled in for the night.

Saegrimr asked Hundolfr, one of the knights sent with the women and children, if he would continue providing some of the basic instruction that had begun that afternoon in the courtyard with one of the sergeants of the muster. Hundolfr agreed, and he spent the next hour instructing the boys about the proper techniques for holding and thrusting their spears. He had them practice bracing the butt of their spears between the ground and the instep of their boots to stop a charging animal and he had them practice forming into ranks to create a layered defense of multiple spears as well as forming a circle to defend from all directions. By the time they finished practicing formations, the last of the daylight had dwindled away and an eerie silence had descended on the hillside. Hundolfr and Olafr organized the men into two hour watches and everyone bedded down for the night. The moon was bright and Amundr was restless, so he passed the time replacing several of his flint arrowheads with the steel ones his father had given him before finally nodding off. He would try to find decent materials to fashion more arrows somewhere along the road.

***

When morning broke, food was doled out quickly and quietly. Nobody got much to eat. Their provisions weren't generous when they started and the women handing out food had heard the speculation from some of the men regarding a longer than expected journey. Aoalbert complained about the quantity and quality of what he did eat, but everyone observed that he ate all that was given to him. Amundr and Saegrimr each shared part of their rations with children around them.

"There are plenty of acorns and other nuts at this time of year." Amundr told Saegrimr "If we were allowed to have a fire I would probably be able to get us a few rabbits and squirrels while we travel, but even I'm not hungry enough to eat them raw." Saegrimr nodded in agreement and they mounted their horses in silence.

Olafr and one of the merchants had returned to the road and scouted a brief distance ahead while the others ate. Now they returned and summoned all the men on horseback together.

"The road seems clear, but the animals are quiet. It's like something has them spooked. Keep your eyes open." He rode down the line and made similar admonitions to the young men riding in the wagons before returning to the front of the line and leading the caravan back down the hill.

***

Olafr rode at the head of the column with a merchant named Fastbjorn, who mostly traded in textiles. Neither one spoke as they set a steady pace towards the south. Hundolfr and Aoalbert rode a few paces behind while the rest of the men rode at the rear of the train in anticipation of pursuit from the vergrinn.

Amundr and Saegrimr weren't sure where to ride. Amundr didn't want to be seen as hanging on his father like a babe and neither he nor Saegrimr had any desire to ride near Aoalbert. At the same time, they didn't quite feel that they truly belonged with the rest of the men at the rear of the column. This was why they were riding near the middle of the column when the vergrinn struck.

The wind had been from the east all morning and the previous day's warmth had been replaced by an autumn chill. After riding along for a couple of leagues, the wind had shifted and the horses had gotten skittish. Suddenly the underbrush to Amundr's right exploded outward and several vergrinn were stabbing and clawing at everything they could reach. Amundr's horse reared and he fell from the saddle. Saegrimr had raised his own horse from a colt and was better able to control him, but even he was having difficulty.

Landing roughly on the ground, Amundr grabbed the spear he had dropped and turned towards the vergrinn. There were five of them – two near Saegrimr and the other three going after one of the wagons. Amundr thrust his spear at a vergrinn between him and his friend, but he missed. He didn't miss by much, and the vergrinn, whose back had been turned, turned to Amundr snarling.

It leapt at Amundr and without thinking Amundr braced his spear as he had done when hunting large animals so many times before. The vergrinn impaled itself on Amundr's spear and the shock from the impact caused it to drop its own, but it still tried to fight its way closer to him. Amundr drew the small axe he carried from his belt and finished the creature off with a flurry of blows.

Amundr wrenched his spear free of the dying brute and turned around to see what was happening. The first thing he saw was his best friend standing alone against a huge vergrinn. Amundr started towards the vergrinn menacing Saegrimr, but cries from the wagons pulled him away. One of the horses pulling the wagon nearest him was on the ground thrashing as blood streamed from the stump of a leg and its stomach. The remaining horses were straining at their harnesses as they tried to flee. The worst image, though, was the remaining vergrinn disappearing back into the underbrush, each clutching a small child in their arms.

Chapter Four

With a shout, Amundr charged after them. He might not be old enough to be considered a man by some, but he knew what the vergrinn would do to those younglings and he wasn't going to stand by and let it happen.

Ahead of him he heard the muffled cries of the children. Behind him he heard frustrated shouts and heavy footsteps running through the forest. Suddenly he burst through a thorny bush and into a clearing where he faced eight vergrinn. The children had been tossed aside and were whimpering at the base of a tree while the vergrinn were all waiting and facing the bushes through which Amundr had just charged.

"It's a trap!" he shouted. The vergrinn bared their fangs and started to maneuver to encircle him cautiously. He was only one man, but he was armed with a spear and the spear still displayed evidence of its recent use.

Amundr backed slowly until he was near the base of a giant oak. He might not be able to take eight vergrinn, but he wouldn't make it easy for them and he intended to make them remember him. His grip tightened around his spear as he backed into the tree trunk. "You want me, come and get me!" he said.

The vergrinn may not have understood his speech, but they clearly understood his meaning. Amundr's spear was positioned to protect against the center of the vergrinn formation, so when the beast to his left was the first to lunge forward Amundr briefly wondered what death would feel like. His thoughts were interrupted by the spears that came out of the bushes to his left and intercepted the charging monster. Several more spears emerged from the bushes to his right and suddenly there were six vergrinn facing eight spearmen and one intimidating knight.

The next thirty seconds flashed by in a blinding swirl of teeth, claws, spears, and Sir Hundolfr's sword. When Amundr paused to catch his breath, all eight vergrinn lay bleeding on the ground along with three of the spearmen and Sir Hundolfr. The spearmen were already dead, and as Fastbjorn cradled Hundolfr's head in his arms the knight gasped with his dying breath "Vergrinn... never smart enough... never patient enough... for something... like... this... Remember... your oaths."

Fastbjorn, who was the least bloody of the survivors, gathered the children together and shepherded them back towards the road. Amundr and the other three spearmen gathered the weapons from the dead. "Where do we bury them?" Amundr asked.

The other three exchanged a look. One of them, Hallr, spoke up. "There is no time. We know that the vergrinn are in these woods but we don't know how many or how close. We can take their gear but we must leave the bodies."

"But they'll be eaten!"

"Lad, if we stop to bury them then the vergrinn will probably catch up with us and eat us. We can't risk a pyre and stones are too few here for a mound. We have no picks or shovels, so digging would take too long. We swore an oath to protect these people. What do you think Sir Hundolfr was trying to tell us before he died?"

Amundr hung his head. They were right, of course. Let the dead bury the dead, the living had more important work to do. He trudged back with them towards the road. Somehow the knowledge that he had fought and slain his enemies didn't outweigh the grief he felt over the loss of his companions.

***

By the time they reached the road, the wagons were almost ready to move out. The horses had been calmed and the minor injuries inflicted upon the children and their defenders had been tended. One of the horses of a fallen spearman had taken the place of the dead cart horse. It wasn't as strong and it was more temperamental, but it was better than not having enough horses and slowing the wagons down. The remaining horses were tethered to the last wagon in line.

Aoalbert was busy trying to sever the head of the vergrinn Amundr had slain. Saegrimr leaned heavily upon his spear as he caught his breath.

"We must move out. Come along milord." Olafr said as he rode up, leading Aoalbert's steed.

"I will have my trophy before we leave."

Olafr's voice dropped to a whisper, "Milord, the only trophies worth taking are the ones you earn yourself."

"You will not speak to me so!" Everyone around fell silent as the youth rebuked the man. Aoalbert regained his composure and spoke again in normal tones. "I will take this trophy so that we may show the Duke the strength in arms of our people. I do this to honor all of us."

Olafr shook his head and kept his voice low. "Sir Hundolfr and the others laid down their lives for us. If we tarry here who will we be laying our lives down for? We will show the Duke our worth by bringing these people to safety.

Aoalbert stood and wiped his bloody sword on the fur of one of the vergrinn corpses. "This beast was far too small to make a decent trophy. I will take the head of a vergrinn worthy of my station. At least we have now met and defeated the vergrinn that had you so worried yesterday evening. We will continue down the road at all speed." He swung astride his horse and proceeded to the head of the column.

***

As Amundr trotted alongside Saegrimr he said "You appear to have done all right."

"I held my ground until your father got there. The others saw you chasing those beasts and took off after you. Hallr said that you got two more in the woods."

"I may have. It was all a blur to me. I have always wanted to be a man. Now that I am here I wish my father could tote me around on his back and tell me that the vergrinn are just a child's bad dream." He sighed as he glanced at the nearest wagon "I fear that no matter how many vergrinn we kill we will not keep them all from their supper. Let's see how long we can delay it."

Chapter Five

They pressed on until midday. They came to an open meadow and stopped to take a meal. The horses were tended and the people all stretched their weary arms and legs. Everyone who had been in the wagon that was attacked was still shaken. The young mother who had been driving that wagon was numb with shock. They moved her and her children to another wagon so that someone else could drive the team.

The equipment retrieved from the dead spearmen was given to three boys who had only seen thirteen winters and they were now asked to stand as men. All of the young men of the muster were distributed more evenly throughout the wagons, occasionally being separated from their families in the process. Every wagon now had two lads and a couple had three, and they were given explicit instructions to watch the sides of the road and keep their spear in their hands.

Once all the people were back in the wagons, Olafr and Fastbjorn led the wagons back onto the road and set a brisk pace. This would tire the horses sooner, but they felt it was urgent to put some distance between them and the battle.

They continued on all afternoon until the sun started going down. None of the men knew of a good defensible place to spend the night near there, so they settled for a small clearing just off the road. They tethered the horses and distributed food. Hundolfr was no longer with them, so Sir Herfinnr, the other knight sent with them, drilled the youngsters in some basic tactics until darkness fell. As the youngsters headed towards their blankets, Amundr thought he saw his father tuck something into the pocket of his jacket. There were fewer men left for the watches that night, so each man was on watch slightly longer.

***

On the second morning, Amundr awoke early and roused Saegrimr. They set off into the woods surrounding their encampment to forage for food. They gathered up as many nuts as they could find along with edible roots and mushrooms and hurried back to the camp as most of the children were waking up. They gave the food they found to the women doling out provisions and accepted their meager breakfast gracefully.

Soon everyone was loaded aboard the wagons and the caravan was back out on the road. The memory of the previous morning hung heavily over the heads of all and the procession was somber and silent. The air was still chilly and the winds began to whip up throughout the day. The previously clear sky was populated with a few clouds. As the day passed, the number of clouds grew. Amundr rode on in silence, thinking about the events of the past few days. He had so many questions and so few answers. At the midday meal break he sought out his father. "Father," he began, keeping his voice low. "What are the vergrinn? Why do they hunt people, and where did they all come from?"

Olafr's eyes shifted from side to side as he looked around at the children, a few of whom appeared to have overheard these questions and were awaiting his response. "They are nothing. We will soon be to Gudmund and free from this danger." He glanced at his son.

As they mounted their horses to get back on the road, Olafr sought Amundr. "Tonight, we will stand the second watch together. Some things are best kept from tender ears in the wild woods."

As Amundr rode along, he realized that for the first time in his life a conversation with his father had left him feeling more frightened and less certain than he had been before. He was anxious to speak with his father again, though, because it was readily apparent that his father knew something significant about the vergrinn.

***

"My father," Olafr began, "fought the vergrinn during the last invasion fifty years ago – back before I was born. I thought that we would have a respite during our lifetimes because never before had the vergrinn attacked in numbers less than a century after being driven back." The two of them were standing on a small outcropping of rock overlooking the camp that night.

"Why did they attack sooner this time?" Amundr asked.

"Good question. Most of the things they've done haven't made any sense. They send out scouts. They strategize. They retreat. They use tools. None of these match the mindless killers that we had seen so many times before. They're attacking in autumn instead of in the deepest, coldest winter. It's almost like these aren't actually vergrinn."

"Well, what's the best way to fight them?"

"If these are the same vergrinn as always, they will be far stronger than men. Their hides are tough. Their hearing, vision, and sense of smell are as keen as those of a wolf. They use spears and their teeth and claws are sharp, deadly weapons."

"Don't they have any weaknesses?"

"They are slower than a man. They are less intelligent than a man. They are more given to fits of battle rage than a man, and they are afraid of fire. They don't like water and they can't swim."

"But where do they come from? What are they?"

Olafr looked long and hard at Amundr as if weighing what to say next. "Some say they are wild animals that have gained a little intelligence. Some say they are a separate type of men. The truth..." a long pause, and when he spoke his voice was no more than a whisper, "The truth is that they are cursed creatures – servants of evil condemned to their fate and constantly hungering after the flesh of men." He spoke with a tone in his voice that indicated that he was not speculating. "The truth is that the vergrinn have existed for thousands of years. They wiped out all men in their ancestral land and eventually found their way here."

"I've never heard that before. How can you know this?"

Another pause. Olafr looked around to ensure no one was near enough to hear. "My father, and his father, and his forefathers before him have passed on the lore of the vergrinn since time immemorial. Whenever they appeared, we have fought to defend the innocent from them and defeat the vergrinn. After the vergrinn were defeated at the battle of the glade, my father settled near there because he was certain that the vergrinn would return. He was right."

"Why have you never told me this?"

"I was going to tell you when you were older. We should have had more time before they returned. You aren't prepared at all, and there is no time to properly prepare you right now. Hopefully we can talk about this more when we get to Gudmund. Our watch is almost over. Get some sleep."

***

The next day the temperature continued to drop. By mid-morning the flurries were falling from the grey sky. As the day wore on, the snow fell faster and faster. By the time they made camp at the side of the road that night there were a few inches of snow on the ground. Many of the children were shivering, and after a hurried consultation it was decided that they would go ahead and light several small fires since the vergrinn hadn't been seen in days.

Since they were going to be using fires for warmth, several of the men went hunting and returned with small game and a deer. These were cooked and shared out among the people. Spirits were higher than they had been since the journey began until the next morning.

Olafr arose early and went out to scout ahead down their path as usual. Upon taking several steps away from the fire he found several tracks in the snow just beyond the reach of the light from their fires. The vergrinn had been here, watching.

Chapter Six

"How many were there?" Aoalbert had been the first to respond to Olafr's call for nearby men, likely because his typical morning involved more eating and less working.

"It looks like there was only one. Judging by his tracks, he arrived after the snow finished falling during the third watch and left before the sun rose this morning."

"How can you tell he left before the sun rose by looking at his tracks?"

"I can't, but this position was downwind until shortly before sunrise when the wind shifted. The horses would have smelled him if he was still here when that happened."

"It can't have gotten far. We should pursue it. We don't want it bringing back more of them."

At this moment, Stigr, who had set off cautiously down the vergrinn's trail, returned. "Milord, I'm more worried about it leading us into another ambush. We've already lost a third of the men your father sent with us and we are still twenty leagues from Gudmund. The vergrinn that was here snuck away for a few yards and then broke into a run. If we are to have any hope of seeing our people to safety and sending help, speed is our best friend."

Aoalbert consented and they set out immediately. The sun rose that morning and the snow melted away. Their mid-day meal break was shortened and they pressed on at the end of the day until the light was almost completely gone. There were no fires tonight after the vergrinn's appearance the night before. The lads drilled briefly and everyone was thoroughly exhausted.

***

The next two days passed unremarkably. The weather was cold and there was light cloud covering, but everyone's spirits were lifted by the fact that they were finally drawing closer to their destination. On the morning of the second day they entered an area that was better described as meadows interrupted by the occasional stand of trees rather than forest interrupted by occasional clearing. Late that afternoon they came out of a band of forest into an open meadow stretching to the horizon. They made camp shortly before sunset and everyone was excited to hear that they should be in Gudmund the next day.

They passed out extra food and held a small feast around several large fires. Stigr, Olafr, and Herfinnr stood off to one side having a quiet discussion. "I'm thankful we have made it this far. I think we have outdistanced the vergrinn and I will be happy to see Gudmund," said Stigr.

Olafr shook his head. "We're almost there, but the vergrinn are persistent. We've been pushing hard, but we're dealing with women and children here. They could be pulling forced marches long into the night. I would hate to get this close and lose our charges." He looked to Herfinnr. "How are the lads coming? They've been training for a week."

Herfinnr hesitated before speaking. "The lads are doing better than you might expect. They know the basics as well as any batch of green recruits, but they're still just lads. If the vergrinn fall on us in full force, who knows what they'll do."

Olafr sighed wearily. "Let's hope we don't have to find out, then."

***

The final day of their journey started out well. They made good time and were soon passing the occasional small cottage off to either side of the road. Every time they passed one of these, Herfinnr or Stigr would ride to the cottage and warn the occupants about the coming of the vergrinn. At the mid-day meal, Stigr and Fastbjorn volunteered to ride ahead and give the villages between there and Gudmund advanced warning so they could withdraw to the city.

On the open plains, Herfinnr and Aoalbert rode at the head of the column while the rest of the men rode at the rear. Saegrimr rode alongside Amundr at the very end of the column and he found it hard to contain his excitement. "Do you think they'll let us stay in the muster now or will we be left out until next summer?"

Amundr shrugged. "It doesn't really matter. We know we belong here. I'd wager that no man of the muster has faced the vergrinn like we have." As soon as he said that, he realized that the men left back at Eyjolf had probably been dealing with vergrinn every day while they were gone and he fell silent.

Saegrimr noticed his friend's silence and changed topics. "Have you ever been to Gudmund? I hear that there are tens of thousands of people there. I wonder what it's like."

Amundr turned to respond, but his attention was drawn away by something he saw out of the corner of his eye. He reined in his horse and turned around for a better view of what was behind them. Not half a league distant on the road he saw several wagons approaching much faster than his own train was traveling. In the distance beyond them he could barely make out a swirling mass of darkness. "Father!"

Olafr was at his side in an instant. "I see them. We'll see what they have to say when they catch up with us."

***

Within half an hour the first of the wagons had caught up with them. "Your man warned us and we gathered our people as quickly as we could. We put most of the children and the elderly in wagons, but many of our people are on foot. They're trying to hurry, but I fear the vergrinn might catch them before we reach the city."

Olafr had a hurried conference with Herfinnr. "Well," began Herfinnr, "I think our best bet is to try to hold them at the bridge over the Svanr River. It is half a mile ahead of us and three leagues from the city gates. You lead the wagons to Gudmund and send back help, while I stay with the men and we hold the bridge against the vergrinn."

Olafr shook his head. "You are known in Gudmund and will be more likely to get help quickly. I will stand with the men. You take Aoalbert and the wagons and fly to safety."

Aoalbert had been sitting on his horse nearby. "I will stay and defend the bridge with the rest of the men. Herfinnr, I order you to get the people to

XLVII

safety. The rest of us will deal with these beasts."
Olafr sighed.

***

They reached the bridge over the Svanr River
in a few minutes. Herfinnr urged the wagons to
hurry and they sped down the road towards
Gudmund. Olafr, Amundr, Saegrimr, Aoalbert, and
four other men remained at the bridge. Each man
had a bow and a quiver of arrows in addition to their
spear. They knew that every minute they could hold
off the vergrinn was another minute when Stigr and
Fastbjorn could be warning villagers between here
and the city.

The stragglers from the outlying villages soon
arrived. They were men and women, old and young.
They were clearly weary already, and the vergrinn
weren't more than a mile behind. If they had all
been healthy adults, they could have outpaced the
vergrinn to Gudmund, but these stood no chance.

Once they had crossed the bridge, Olafr
organized the hasty construction of a barricade on
the northern end of the bridge to slow the vergrinn.
They used logs, branches and stones they had
dragged up from the surrounding creek bed while
waiting for the stragglers. They hurried back across
the bridge and arranged a similar barricade there.

By now the vergrinn were no more than two
furlongs away. Olafr encouraged his men.

"Remember, we can start shooting them as soon as they get within range. Once they cross the far barricade, lay aside your bow and ready your spear. The bridge is narrow enough that if we stand together we can hold it for a long time."

The vergrinn kept coming. The men could hear their howls and growls as they hurried towards the bridge. It seemed to Amundr as if the presence of the defenders enraged the vergrinn and motivated them to move even faster. Soon they were within bowshot. Every one of the defenders started firing arrows as fast as they could into a crowd of vergrinn so large it seemed impossible to miss. Arrow after arrow found its mark and the number of the vergrinn who were falling rose.

There were at least three score vergrinn down when the first vergrinn got to the barricade at the north end of the bridge, yet there were still hundreds coming. As they began to clamber over the barricades Amundr and the others kept shooting. It was working! The bridge was narrow enough and the barricade stout enough that the vergrinn would not be able to pass.

Suddenly a howl and a growling voice rose above the rest. The defenders kept shooting while the front ranks of vergrinn pulled back and several vergrinn with axes came forward and started hacking away at the barricade. The vergrinn would be through the northern barricade any minute, but that didn't matter as the defenders were almost out of arrows. Seven score vergrinn had been felled by the defenders' arrows when their last was fired. Amundr had used all of his new steel ones as well as his older flint arrows.

The barrier was finally down and the vergrinn pressed their way across the bridge. The men held their spears ready, a hint of nervousness present in all of them. "Stand firm," Olafr admonished, "Every minute we hold them here saves innocent lives."

The defenders held the end of the bridge for what seemed like hours. Thrust. Slash. Stab. Parry. Amundr's arms wearied with the effort. The vergrinn dead piled higher and still they kept coming. A spear slipped through and got one of the defenders in the leg. He went down with a cry. Another man was stabbed through the chest. Aoalbert had his spear wrenched from his grasp and he was suddenly fleeing to the horses which were tethered twenty yards to the west of the bridge. "They're scaling the banks!" he shouted. Several dozen vergrinn had snuck down the far bank of the river and laid logs from the barricade across a narrow portion of the river and were now climbing the bank near the horses.

"Fly!" cried Olafr. "We can hold them no longer. To the city!" He stood with Amundr, Saegrimr, and two other men. Amundr and Saegrimr stood by Olafr, but the two other men headed for the horses. After Aoalbert had mounted his horse and fled, the other horses had pulled their stakes and followed. The two men heading towards where the horses had been tethered were soon swallowed amongst dozens of vergrinn.

"Head down the river to the coast, then follow it south to the city!" Olafr shouted at the boys. The barrier was now all but unguarded and the vergrinn were almost over. Olafr dove in front of a spear intended for Amundr and said "GO! You are... the last... wolf spear..."

Chapter Seven

Saegrimr grabbed Amundr by the arm and ran. They were both numbed by what had just happened. Amundr's father had been the bravest man they knew. He slew wolves, boars, and the largest of bears alone and armed with a spear, and now he was dead. They ran as fast as they could, with the howling and growling pursuing them every step of the way. Neither of them knew how far the coast was, but they both knew what would happen the minute they stopped running.

Amundr noticed the howling growing slightly fainter and remembered what his father had said about vergrinn not being quite as fast as a man. He dared to look behind him and saw that they were now almost a hundred yards ahead of their pursuers. It didn't look like they had more than a dozen pursuers, but those were sufficient numbers to be the end of Amundr and Saegrimr, both of whom had dropped their spears in those first panicked moments of flight.

"Little Mundi... how far... do you think... we'll have to run?"

"Not sure... Ask them if... they're getting tired...."

"No thanks."

They looked ahead and saw their way barred by a tributary flowing into the Svanr. Amundr's heart leapt as he remembered that vergrinn couldn't swim. "Come on, we'll be fine if we hurry!"

They leapt into the frigid water and swam across the narrow river. It was probably almost shallow enough to flounder across without really swimming, but Amundr didn't want to think about that. They reached the far bank and saw that the vergrinn were almost to the opposite bank. They took a moment to catch their breath and watched as the vergrinn approached very hesitantly. They weren't going in the water!

"Ha! They don't want to get wet!" Saegrimr crowed. His teeth were chattering with the cold now. "All the same, we ought to keep moving so that when they do figure out a way across we are long gone." Amundr agreed and they set out down the river towards the coast, walking this time.

***

After walking along for almost half an hour, the two boys started to hear the distant cry of gulls and knew they were nearing the coast. A large tree had apparently been uprooted and was lying with the base of its trunk across their path and the top of the tree on the far side of the Svanr River.

The boys were too cold and tired to try to scramble over the thick trunk, so they worked their way around it to the right. As they got to the point where the trunk had snapped off, they stopped. Sticking out of the ground in the middle of a hole in what had been the trunk was a sword in an old, worn scabbard. There was something attached to the sword, but they couldn't figure out what it was. Something about it made Saegrimr nervous. "We should leave it alone. It just feels like magic."

Amundr disagreed, "It does feel like magic, but it also feels right. I'm going to take it." He walked over to the sword and tried to pull it free, but the sword wouldn't budge. He removed a metal canister that had been attached to the hilt of the sword with rusty wire and tried again. Still no luck.

"I told you we should leave it alone."

"My hands are just too slippery and cold." Amundr removed his gloves to get a better grip on the hilt. As soon as his fingers tightened around the hilt, the sword slid out of the ground as if it were a knife sliding through the ripest pear. The two boys looked at each other in shock.

"Let's keep moving," said Saegrimr, and they started back along the river towards the coast.

Amundr paused briefly to put his gloves back on before picking up the sword and continuing.

***

They reached the coast without further incident. The sun was fading behind them when they encountered a small fishing village where the river ran into the sea. A few folks were out mending nets and sealing boats with pitch as the boys walked up, and a low murmur arose among them.

Amundr turned to Saegrimr to speak and immediately realized how they must look. They had been covered in blood and fur and filth, then dunked into a frigid river and walked the rest of the way here. Before either of them could speak a voice called out, "Who are you and why are you here?"

The two boys turned towards a small hut. In the doorway stood an elderly man, leaning upon a staff. Saegrimr spoke up, "If you please, sir, you must get your people together and go to Gudmund. The vergrinn have returned."

All around were silent for a moment, then the murmur returned, louder than before. "Vergrinn, you say? Lads, such things are not a topic for jesting," the old man said. "Vergrinn haven't been seen in fifty years, and their harbingers are two boys not old enough to stand as men? I think not."

Amundr was perfectly content to let Saegrimr speak again. His father was a village elder and he knew more about dealing with such folk. "Sir, we are from Eyjolf. The vergrinn set upon us and we were sent with the women and children to Gudmund for our protection. Thrice the vergrinn came upon us on the road, and the last time my companion and I stood with six others to hold the bridge over the Svanr against the beasts while the others fled for safety. All of our companions fell, and the last was my companion's father who told us to flee down the river and make our way to the city. There were a dozen or so vergrinn behind us an hour ago, but they wouldn't cross that small river that fed into the Svanr."

More silence followed. Finally the elder spoke again, "I hear the truth in your voices. If the vergrinn were behind you they are still pursuing. We will all withdraw to the city." He immediately began issuing orders to the men and women around to prepare their boats and load them with supplies. Two men were sent throughout the village to ensure everyone heard the news and was prepared to leave. A long howling rose in the distance.

"We'd better leave soon." The elder said.

Chapter Eight

The villagers soon had their boats laden with supplies and people and they headed out to sea. As they sped towards the open water, Amundr and Saegrimr looked back and saw the forms of vergrinn in the village. The vergrinn let out howls of frustration and the villagers looked back in dismay and fear.

"We don't usually take the boats out at night when it's this cloudy, so we'll stay closer to the shore so we can navigate," said the middle aged man at the tiller of their boat. "It's a little riskier because of the rocks closer to the shoreline, but far better than being swept out to sea. Sky looks like it'll have another storm for us tomorrow. That has given us one good thing – the wind has shifted around to the north and will drive us where we want to go pretty quick."

Amundr and Saegrimr remained silent. Neither had spent any time on a boat other than paddling up and down small rivers in a canoe. Finally Amundr spoke up. "How long until we get to Gudmund?"

"Less than an hour. We go there to trade all the time, but we stay here because the fishing is better near the mouth of the river. There's lots more people in Gudmund too, and most of us don't take too kindly to strangers."

The sun was almost completely down at this point, and as Amundr looked over at the shore he could barely make out the forms of several vergrinn. They were shadowing the progress of the ship, but with a stiff wind at their backs the fishing vessels quickly outpaced them.

***

The journey seemed to fly by. The smell of the salt air and the cry of the gulls was a new and wonderful experience for the two lads from the woods near Eyjolf. They felt refreshed and invigorated. Before long, a faint golden glow shone like a halo around the trees ahead and to their right. They rounded a bend of the shore and the lights of the city of Gudmund sprang up before them. The city's outer walls went down to the shore and even extended into the shallows beyond. They were made of stone, but they looked as smooth as the stones from the bottom of a creek instead of giant blocks of hewn rock. The pennants waving from the walls looked like giant blue and white party decorations, stiffened by the steady wind.

Saegrimr spoke first. "I wonder if the others made it here." Amundr's heart sank. For the past hour he had been so lost in the joy of his first sea trip that he had forgotten their urgent flight and even the death of his father.

"I hope Aoalbert got eaten. If I see him he'll wish he had."

"Mundi, be reasonable. Sure, he's a cowardly fool, but he's also a noble. If you lay a hand on him you'll be in prison until they kill you." He paused, then continued. "Actually, if Aoalbert hadn't been such a coward the vergrinn would have snuck up on all of us unawares and we'd all have been killed. That doesn't make him a hero, but it does make you think."

The fisher folk entered a harbor protected by a stout sea wall. Men on the docks called out greetings with a curious tone in their voice. One called to the elder in the front boat. "Gedda, what brings you here so late?"

"Vergrinn. They came upon us at sunset, and we would have all been lost but for a warning from some well met visitors."

"We had heard of the coming of the vergrinn and were going to send someone to you in the morning. We didn't think they would travel all the way to your village at the shore so soon."

"Well, our well met visitors may have led them there. They apparently met them earlier in the day at the Svanr bridge."

Even in the dim light, the surprise on the stranger's face was evident. "We heard news from the Svanr bridge. Your visitors ought to go to the citadel at once."

***

The boats were pulled ashore on a sandy beach and tied to rings set in heavy posts. Amundr and Saegrimr were introduced to Igull, who had greeted them on the docks. "I'll take you up to the citadel."

They walked through the broad streets of the city. Even at night they were impressed by the size and variety of everything. The streets were so wide that two wagons could go through side by side, and every building had two stories or more. They passed a courtyard where their church building could have been placed comfortably with both of their houses beside it.

Igull was apparently known in the citadel. At the entrance to the citadel, one of the guards simply glanced at him and waved them in. They passed under the portcullis and into a courtyard larger than the one they had passed previously. Igull opened a large wooden door directly across the courtyard from the portcullis and turned right down a long hallway.

Amundr and Saegrimr could hear noises coming from down the hall and as they got closer they could begin to make out voices. Igull paused at an open doorway to his left, and the boys were standing behind him.

From across the hall they heard an exclamation. "Amundr! Saegrimr! You live!" The sound in the hall died down as Sir Herfinnr, Fastbjorn, and Stigr rushed over to greet them. "We had heard that all fell defending the bridge save Aoalbert." Herfinnr grinned as he said this.

"My father fell. All who stood and fought fell save Saegrimr and I." There was a bitterness in Amundr's voice that none could mistake. "At the last there were three of us. As my father fell he ordered us to flee down the river. The good people there brought us here." They were not much more presentable than they had been at the fishing village, but each of the older men took them into a warm embrace.

"We will speak of Aoalbert later," said Herfinnr. For now, let us get you cleaned and fed. The young men allowed themselves to be led from the chamber to a room where hot baths and fresh clothes were laid out for them. They undressed and bathed, then hastily redressed and left the chamber. Amundr brought with him the sword and canister he had found within the tree. They found a man waiting to take them back to the hall, where the feast was still underway.

***

They were seated at a table near their traveling companions and they dug in hungrily to the food provided for them. The two young lads, who had been on short rations for a week, showed the rest of the diners in the hall the meaning of the word ravenous.

After they had each had a fourth helping of everything, they finally slowed their eating. "Did the wagons make it through safely? Did you warn the other villagers? Did the other villagers come to harm? Are we setting out tomorrow for Eyjolf" The questions came tumbling out of both of them so fast that Stigr held up a hand to silence them.

"One question at a time, lads. I believe the first was whether the wagons made it through safely?" Both lads nodded. "Yes, the wagons made it through. Herfinnr saw to that. All the lads aboard looked nervous as a pie at a party, but they made it through."

"What of the other villages? Did they get warned in time?" Amundr asked.

Stigr nodded. "Fastbjorn and I warned every village this side of the Svanr and many on the far side. Well, every village not on the coast. Those were a bit far afield and we thought they'd be safe until boats could get to them tomorrow. As for the villagers, every one of them from the villages we warned got to the city in safety. You boys did well holding that bridge. The vergrinn had almost reached the stragglers from the last villages when the sortie the Duke sent out got there. They mopped up every one of the vergrinn and went back to the bridge to recover the bodies. We thought you two had ended up in the river and been washed out to sea. They counted the vergrinn and there were over ten score dead at that bridge. The bards will sing of that battle." Amundr thought of his father's fate and wished there hadn't been any battle for the bards to sing of. "Several of the horsemen continued up the road to make sure that there weren't any more large groups of vergrinn coming. It looks like there may be a few scattered here and there but no organized forces back to the edge of the wood."

Saegrimr asked "And will we set out for Eyjolf tomorrow?"

Stigr and Fastbjorn looked to Herfinnr. "We will set out soon, but not tomorrow. The Duke was able to send out six score of mounted knights in the sortie, and that was sufficient for the three hundreds of vergrinn that remained after they crossed the bridge, but your father's men said there were at least two thousands of the vergrinn. The Duke has called out the muster throughout the duchy. It may take several days for the men to arrive and be provisioned. As soon as the muster is ready a force will be sent, and it may be three thousand spears or more." Amundr had never heard of three thousand men fighting in one battle. The thought overwhelmed him.

"What of Aoalbert? Clearly he survived. Will his cowardice go unpunished?" Amundr asked the question out of bitterness and anger.

It was Herfinnr who spoke. "For now, Aoalbert is being treated with the benefits befitting his station. Fear not, the truth of the battle at Svanr Bridge will be known." Herfinnr looked up at the high table on the dais at the end of the hall. It took Amundr a moment to realize that Aoalbert was sitting up there at the Duke's own table!

Chapter Nine

Amundr fumed silently for the remainder of the feast. When the feast ended, Stigr said "Come, we will show you where you are sleeping." Stigr and Fastbjorn took their leave of Herfinnr and left the great hall with Amundr and Saegrimr. "As a knight, Herfinnr is entitled to a small chamber of his own in the keep. We are staying in the barracks with other men of the muster," Stigr explained.

The group went back out the entrance and entered one of the buildings on the side of the courtyard. They went up a winding staircase to a wooden door. Past the door the stairs continued upwards into the darkness. Stigr opened the door and said "Welcome home, boys."

They stepped in and saw that they were at one end of a long room with stone walls and a wooden floor. There were perhaps three score low beds in two rows running the length of the room and beside each bed was a small trunk. A few torches shone dimly in sconces set at regular intervals down the length of the left-hand wall and there was a fire burning in a fireplace in the middle of the same wall.

The wall on the right had four narrow windows which were currently shuttered against the chill night air and Amundr realized they probably overlooked the courtyard. Roughly half of the bunks appeared to be occupied, mostly those closest to the fireplace or furthest from the windows.

Some of the room's current occupants were whittling, a few were sharpening weapons, a small circle of onlookers had formed around one pair who were wrestling. Past those Amundr saw that two were praying and one had some parchment out and appeared to be writing something.

Amundr and Saegrimr immediately recognized the room's current occupants as the rest of the boys from their muster. As they made their way into the room, Fastbjorn called out to the boys already present "New recruits boys, fresh in from the road. Don't be too hard on them." Then to Amundr and Saegrimr he added "You two grab whichever bunks you like so long as they're not already taken."

All of the boys looked up as Amundr and Saegrimr slowly walked to the unoccupied bunks closest to the warmth of the fireplace and a murmur arose. "It's Amundr and Saegrimr! They're supposed to be dead! What happened? Tell us everything!"

The boys all crowded around the newcomers and finally Stigr said "Alright you lads. Let them breathe. If we're going to listen to the story, let's gather around the fire where it's warm. It's a little scary. So take care it doesn't give you nightmares as you're men of the muster now and you're moms aren't here to hold you in the middle of the night." Saegrimr, who was always better with words and more comfortable with people, related their tale to their rapt audience, and then answered various questions about their adventure that the boys asked.

After a while Stigr told them all it was time to get to sleep. "You've had a long few days and it's just beginning. We're going to train you lads up and when the Duke sends his spearmen marching to Eyjolf's rescue I want every one of you ready to march there with them." The boys went to their beds, but Stigr's comments left an excited buzz in the air that didn't die down for quite a while.

As Amundr lay in bed, the enormity of the situation finally overwhelmed him. His father had been his best friend and constant companion since his mother passed away when he was just a lad, and now his father was gone! What would become of their home? What would become of him? He rolled onto his side, facing away from the other lads and the warmth of the hearth. He tried to stifle the sobs that wracked his body until he finally fell asleep, exhausted and numb.

On the next bunk over, Saegrimr listened quietly. He didn't think any of the other lads were paying attention, and he was too confused to know what to do. He resolved to pretend he had heard nothing to avoid embarrassing his friend.

***

The lads from Eyjolf all arose fairly early the next morning. They washed in cold water from a rain barrel and ate a plain breakfast of grain mush, toasted bread, and milk. After breakfast they all dressed and went down to the church to worship. At worship, Saegrimr's mother Hafbera and his younger brothers and sisters came over and hugged him, thrilled that he was not nearly as dead as they had been told. When worship was over, the lads returned to their barracks, had a quick meal, grabbed their spears, and headed down to the courtyard to drill.

The recruits were put through their paces by a grizzled man at arms with a long scar across his face that was interrupted by the patch over his left eye. The scar continued down to the left side of his mouth and appeared to have frozen his face in a permanent scowl. After half an hour of exercising, he paused as he saw Herfinnr crossing the courtyard towards him.

"I need to take these two away for a few minutes," Herfinnr said, indicating Amundr and Saegrimr.

"Sure, take them. None of these kids can fight worth anything anyway. Take them all, and then when they're out there bleeding and dying remember that I tried to teach them and you interrupted. Go ahead and take them and get out of here." None of the lads had been around long enough to realize that this was just his way of teasing new recruits, so several of them were more than a little nervous.

"Thanks. I'll get them back to you as soon as I can." Herfinnr gestured to Amundr and Saegrimr and they followed him back toward the Duke's hall.

***

Herfinnr led the boys back to the main hall. A large fire burned in the hearth and several lanterns produced a soft, warm glow throughout the room. The Duke was a large man – taller than any of the men of Eyjolf – and he was standing and talking to several men when Herfinnr led them in. His beard was graying and Amundr thought he must have seen a few more winters than his own father. When he saw Herfinnr leading the boys in, the Duke ended his conversation and strode over to them. His broad smile radiated warmth and good humor.

"Well met indeed. I have heard the full story of your journey from Sir Herfinnr. Never before have I heard of such great deeds being done by such young men." Men! Amundr thought. He speaks of us as men, not boys.

Saegrimr spoke up. "Thank you, your lordship. We just tried to do what was right. We had no ambition for greatness."

The Duke smiled again. "There's a lesson in that. When men set out to seek honor and glory they often ignore virtue to receive what they seek. When they set out to do what is right they often find that honor follows after. Never forget that. Nevertheless, you have served my people well and have thus served me well. Any man that displays such courage and strength at arms should be rewarded." Amundr and Saegrimr looked at each other in stunned disbelief.

"Your honor, we seek no reward. Others paid the full measure to save us both. They and their families should be rewarded." As Saegrimr said this, Amundr nodded. Many had died protecting their people.

"Others have earned honor and they shall indeed receive it," the Duke continued. "Their families will receive tokens of our appreciation as well. You, however, have also earned the reward I am bestowing upon you, though you may come to think it more burdensome over time. Kneel."

Both Amundr and Saegrimr dropped to one knee. The Duke drew his sword from its scabbard and tapped them each on both shoulders. "For valor in combat, for virtue in conduct, and for honor received, I grant you the rank of Knight of the Order of the Rock. You are now a protector of the kingdom of Alarr and the duchy of Gudmund. Repeat after me."

The Duke led them as they swore fealty to him, the duchy, the kingdom, and the king. They swore to protect the people and to always act with honor and courage. When it was done he said "Now rise, Sir Amundr of Eyjolf and Sir Saegrimr of Eyjolf." They rose, and he clasped their hands before pulling each of them into a warm embrace. Herfinnr, who had been watching silently, smiled and patted each of them on the back. "Now Herfinnr," the Duke continued, "Take these two to the quartermaster and see that they are outfitted as befits their station."

He seemed to notice for the first time the sword Amundr had been carrying with him since he found it the day before. "What is this?" Amundr told the tale of how they had found it in the stump of the tree and the Duke's eyebrows shot up in curiosity. "May I take it and examine it? The canister as well?" Something deep inside him made Amundr hesitant to relinquish the sword, but he nodded. He handed the items to the Duke. "I will call on the lore masters and we will see what we can discover about these." He nodded to all of them and strode from the hall.

***

As the two new knights watched the Duke depart, their minds reeled at their sudden change of fortune. Herfinnr noticed their confused looks and spoke up. "Well, come with me. There are a lot of things you need to do now that you are knights."

Amundr and Saegrimr followed as Herfinnr and one of the Duke's household knights led them through the corridors of the keep. "The first thing we need to do is get you some more equipment," said Herfinnr.

The other knight opened a heavy wooden door and took a torch from a wall sconce. "Let's see if we have any armor that will fit you." He led the way into the room, where Amundr and Saegrimr saw shelves laden with musty leather garments and shields. On the far wall they saw various items hanging from hooks embedded in the stone. There was a large barrel full of unstrung bows and another filled with spears. There were boxes full of wooden arrow shafts already formed and a box filled with steel arrowheads. "The Duke has decreed that you shall be outfitted at his personal expense. We were able to retrieve some of what you left behind at the river, but as knights you are now entitled to wear and wield swords."

Herfinnr picked up a stout leather jerkin with mail rings embedded in the front and back and held it up to Saegrimr. "If we tighten the laces, this should fit you well enough." He helped Saegrimr into the jerkin and tightened it. "How does that feel? Can you move your arms? Can you breathe?" Saegrimr indicated that he could and Herfinnr repeated the entire process with Amundr. He then proceeded to help them find and fit heavy leather pants and topped each of them off with a steel helm.

The helmets were a little large and tended to twist sideways so that their view was blocked, but the older knights found some rags and used them to pad the helmets properly in order to keep them in place.

They were each given a sword and a shield. "We'll show you how to use those later," they were assured. Finally Herfinnr said "Now we will go gather the remainder of your things."

They were led back through the corridors to the courtyard, where they found themselves to be the center of attention. "Nobody this young has been knighted in Gudmund in years," their escort explained. Even their young companions from the muster of Eyjolf stopped their practicing to watch, which drew a rebuke from their grizzled instructor.

They entered a building adjacent to their barracks where several piles of gear were laid on tables. "I believe that's yours," Herfinnr said to Saegrimr, gesturing at the first pile of equipment. "And that pile is yours," he said to Amundr, gesturing at the next pile.

The pile of gear looked larger than Amundr had been expecting. "Sir, there must be some mistake."

"We are equals now. You may call me Herfinnr. There has been no mistake. Your father's things are there as well." Herfinnr and the other knight stepped outside, leaving Amundr and Saegrimr alone.

Amundr fought tears as he went through the pile of equipment. He picked up the knife that his father used to show him how to skin animals. The water skin they had shared on many occasions was here, but it had been torn open. He looked through the pile, suddenly simply not caring about any of these dead things. His eyes fell upon the fleece lined jacket his father had worn for as long as Amundr could remember. He gently lifted it out of the pile and buried his face in it and breathed deeply, remembering being held close in his father's arms after his mother's passing.

He felt something inside one of the pockets of the jacket. He took it out and saw that it was several sheets of parchment folded tightly together. He slowly unfolded the parchment and laid it across the table to smooth it out.

"What's that?" inquired Saegrimr.

"I'm not sure. My father taught me to read when I was little, but I didn't think he was much for reading or writing." They brought the parchment closer to the light streaming through the window to the courtyard and they read it.

Chapter Ten

Immediately upon leaving the great hall, the Duke headed towards the library. The city and citadel of Gudmund had been established almost as long ago as the capital, and the founders had insisted on creating an archive of knowledge. At some point in the past the city had been rebuilt at its present location and the library had been moved. The Duke had recognized the metal canister as a scroll tube as soon as he had seen it. It was sturdier than most and had been subjected to the elements, but its contents might still be of use.

He burst into the large, well lit library. "My lord," the elderly lore master began, "My apprentice and I have been researching the vergrinn as you requested. The records of their past incursions are somewhat scattered, but we have found the Official Chronicles of the duchy that pertain to several of the most recent incursions."

"Excellent. Before you do anything else about that, I have something for you to examine." He presented the scroll tube to one of the men, keeping the sword Amundr had discovered tucked under his other arm.

"Your lordship, this is astounding." The scroll tube was made of silver, long blackened with age. Its cap was also silver and it had been sealed with molten lead. Imprinted in the middle of the lead were two runes – the rune of the duchy of Gudmund and an unknown rune that resembled the letter U. "Where did this come from?"

"If the story I was told is correct, it was inside a rather old tree near the banks of the Svanr River. I would like to be able to know what it says as soon as possible."

"Certainly, sir." The two men scurried about the library, gathering various tools. They brought the scroll tube to a table and laid it down. The lore master's apprentice held the tube steady while the master himself retrieved a small hammer and chisel from the pile of tools they had assembled. He delicately chipped away at the lead seal, artfully avoiding the runes in the metal so that they could be preserved for study.

After several minutes, the last of the lead had fallen away from the tube. The lore master tugged and twisted on the tube's cap, worrying it loose like a child's tooth. The cap finally came free, and the lore master pulled a vellum scroll from inside the tube. He laid it out on the table and began to examine it.

"It's written in a slightly older dialect," he began. "I imagine this scroll was written several hundred years ago." Pausing as he looked over the scroll, he finally began reading.

We have defeated the vergrinn yet again, but at a great cost. I am weary to the bone and do not know if I will recover from my wounds. My sons are all dead save the youngest, and he lies dying in the citadel at Gudmund in the care of Ulfbane. I fear the Wolf Spears may no longer protect the land. I am entrusting the sword of the Spears to this place. The place has known power for good and will keep the sword until one arises who may draw and wield it.

Aleifr

The three men were silent. Finally, the apprentice turned to the Duke and spoke. "Is that the sword as mentioned in this scroll?" He gestured at the sword the Duke had under his arm. The Duke shrugged. He held the sword out for the lore master and his apprentice to see. "May we examine it?" The Duke handed it over. The lore master laid it on the table and they wiped it down with cloths. Cleaned and viewed in the light, intricate scrollwork was plainly visible on the scabbard as well as the crosspiece of the blade itself. At the center of both was the same unknown rune from the scroll case. "May we draw it and examine the blade?"

The Duke again nodded. The lore master tried to pull the blade free of its scabbard, but it wouldn't budge. The apprentice tried as well, to no avail. The Duke himself attempted to withdraw the blade from its scabbard and found that he could not. "I wonder…" he murmured.

"Your Lordship, we mentioned that we had found information on the vergrinn in the archives."

"Yes, and?"

"Well, you ought to read some of it now." The lore master looked to his apprentice, who nodded vigorously. "It deals with a legendary group of men known as the 'Wolf Spears'…"

***

Amundr's heart leapt as he looked down at the page. This was something his father had written specifically for him! He read the first sheet.

Amundr,

I had thought we would have more time. The vergrinn are coming and we are about to depart for Gudmund. You know nothing of our heritage or lineage, and that can't be corrected yet. I have a sense of great foreboding, and I am writing this in case I do not make it to Gudmund.

We are the Wolf Spears. Our ancestors were the first to stand against the vergrinn in time out of mind. We have acquired some small knowledge about them, but much was lost hundreds of years ago when our line almost died out during the eighth vergrinn war. We have no special strength at arms, but through some power we are able to understand the foul speech of the vergrinn. Our ancestors swore an oath to stand against the vergrinn when all others fled, and we have quietly watched and waited for every incursion they have made. They are calling for us to mount up. There is no more time to write any more now. I'll make sure we can talk on our trip.

Father

Saegrimr was looking at him guiltily. He clearly felt that he had intruded in something deeply personal between Amundr and his father. "I'll just step over here," he said. "You can finish reading without me." Saegrimr went and gathered the rest of his gear from the pile on the table and walked out the door. Amundr simply nodded and turned to the next page.

Amundr,

Today you fought like a man. Your friend Saegrimr did well today, but none matched you. When I saw you tear off into the woods to help those children my heart swelled with pride. How you have helped the powerless! How you have saved the arm that is feeble! You will be a great Spear, I only wish that you didn't have to live through one of the vergrinn wars. If you always remember that it is our duty to protect those that are weaker, you won't go wrong. The righteous will hold to their ways, and those with clean hands will grow stronger.

Father

Amundr's hands were trembling slightly as he picked up the third and final sheet of parchment.

Amundr,

We spoke briefly last night of the vergrinn. I didn't want to frighten the children, but I also didn't want to frighten you. They are foul creatures. They are cursed. As you stand against them, always remember:

"Those who hate me without reason outnumber the hairs of my head; many are my enemies without cause, those who seek to destroy me."

They will ignore cattle and game and horses to eat human flesh, and they even eat their own dead. They are ferocious fighters, but they are slow-witted and not swift of foot. My father told me that while he was fighting the last vergrinn war, he heard that in the archives at Gudmund there was information about the vergrinn and the Wolf Spears that might be helpful. I intended to take you there when you were older, but hopefully we will be there in a few days. I hope you never have to read these notes, but I fear that you will.

Father

     Amundr folded the letters back up and put them in his pocket. He started inventorying arrows and checking his bow. He heard the door to the courtyard open again and thought Saegrimr must have come back in to check on him. "I'm almost done here. I'll be along in a minute."

     "That will be fine." It wasn't Saegrimr's voice. Amundr looked up and saw the Duke standing in the doorway looking at him. "We need to talk."

Chapter Eleven

The Duke led Amundr into a small chamber with no windows and a single door. He set the lantern he had brought with him on a table and pulled up a chair. He laid the sword on the table before him and asked Amundr to take a seat opposite him.

"So. Amundr. I have been talking to the lore master and I wanted to ask you a few questions." Amundr sat on the edge of his seat, hanging on every word. "First of all, I'd like for both of us to look at this blade a little more closely. Would you mind drawing it out and holding it in the light where we can see it?"

Amundr consented. He picked up the sword with the hilt in his right hand and the scabbard in his left and smoothly drew the blade. The light of the lamp cast a wavering gleam on the metal, and Amundr's eyes could barely make out a wavering line down the length of the blade. The blade was curved like a cavalry saber, and it appeared that its long rest within the tree had neither dulled the shine nor the edge of the metal. In what must have been a trick of the light, the blade looked almost blood red.

"Amazing," the Duke murmured. Amundr agreed, not realizing that the primary source of the Duke's astonishment was the boy's ability to draw the blade, not the craftsmanship evident in the blade. "Tell me Amundr, have you ever heard of the term 'Wolf Spear'?"

The Duke could tell by the way Amundr started that he had indeed heard the term before. "I will tell you what I have learned from our archives and you can tell me what you know." Amundr nodded.

"Our kingdom enjoyed peace and prosperity from its founding until the first vergrinn war. On one fateful day over a thousand years ago, the land went through an upheaval and the isthmus where we are now sitting was thrust up from the ocean floor, connecting two islands together. That winter, a wave of vergrinn crossed the isthmus from the north and terrorized our people."

Amundr had never heard this before. Apparently his father had been correct in thinking that the archives at Gudmund held information on the vergrinn. The Duke continued.

"Since that time, there have been eleven wars fought with the vergrinn. This citadel was established after the seventh vergrinn war to provide a first line of defense against vergrinn incursions. After the ninth vergrinn war we constructed the wall that extends into the ocean to the farthest point that is covered by pack ice in the winters. After the eleventh vergrinn war, we founded the town of Eyjolf to provide a haven in the land of the north for settlers as well as to provide an early warning of trouble with the vergrinn."

"It seems to have done its job well," Amundr offered.

"Yes, it has. All of those facts are from the Official Chronicles of the duchy of Gudmund. As the lore master looked elsewhere in the archives, he found additional information. Apparently, from the time of the first vergrinn war through the time of the eighth vergrinn war there was a group of individuals known as Wolf Spears or occasionally just Spears. These men were always on the front line and were always extremely effective in fighting the vergrinn. They often even brought advanced warning that the vergrinn were coming once again. There is a record of many of these spears falling in the eighth vergrinn war and there is no record of their existence since then."

The Duke paused, watching Amundr. Amundr was looking down at the table, clearly lost in thought. "Amundr," the Duke began. Amundr looked up at the Duke. "Are you a Wolf Spear?"

Amundr didn't know what to say. He wished for the thousandth time that his father was still here. It was his father that the Duke should be talking to, not Amundr. Amundr shrugged. "I am." He went on to explain that he had never heard the term until his father told him he was a Wolf Spear with his dying breath and that he had not known that the group existed until a few days before.

The Duke spoke again. "This is glad tidings indeed. One thing I have not told you is that there was another thread woven through the histories. Until the eighth vergrinn war, the Wolf Spears were always led by a powerful warrior with a unique blood red blade. The warriors and the blade disappeared from our stories centuries ago at the end of the eighth war, but they appear to have both been found in time for this one. This will bring great hope to the people. The sword is yours, apparently by birthright. Several of us tried and failed to draw it, yet it knew your hand. Bear it well, young Spear."

The Duke was rising as if to leave. Amundr didn't want to miss his chance to ask a few questions. "Your lordship?"

"Yes, Amundr?"

"How long until the relief force is sent to Eyjolf?"

"We will depart in three days." At Amundr's questioning look the Duke continued, "Yes, I said 'we' will depart. I do not lead my men by sitting safe in my keep while they march out to shed their blood, and if I understand correctly now seems to be the time that was ordained for you to step forward into the role of a man. You will be instructed in the use of knightly weapons for the rest of your time here and then you will join us in the march to Eyjolf."

"Thank you, milord. If I may ask one last question, what of the other boys – I mean men from Eyjolf. They are all training hard and would all be loathe to remain behind."

"At the very least Aoalbert shall remain behind. Strategic withdrawal in the face of overwhelming odds is usually acceptable, but abandoning your comrades is not. As for the others, if old Adiarfr says they are ready, they can go. I remember being young and willing to shed blood, thinking that it would be the other fellow's instead of my own. Let's get you back to the others."

***

The Duke brought Amundr back out to the courtyard, where Adiarfr and his young charges were taking a midday meal in the open air. As they got closer, Amundr could hear snatches of conversation.

"They made Amundr and Saegrimr knights! Can you believe it?"

"Of course they made them knights. They stood against hundreds of vergrinn and slew dozens of them each!"

"I heard they each slew over a hundred!"

At this point the voice of the grizzled instructor Adiarfr interrupted. "They each did their part. I am sure by this time tomorrow they will have stood against a thousand and slain five hundreds each and by this time next year they will have repelled the entire vergrinn force and saved your town with nothing but a stern glance. Whatever they did or did not do, it is time for all of you to return to your practicing so that each of you can do your part."

With a collective groan the young men picked up their spears and shields and formed ranks in the courtyard. As Amundr walked over to where Herfinnr and Saegrimr were engaged in swordplay with wooden swords, the Duke caught Adiarfr's eye and beckoned him over. "Will they be ready when we leave in three days?"

Adiarfr lowered his voice. "Well, they've got more spirit than most green recruits and they've learned the basics as fast as any group I've trained. They need a few more seasons to really be able to put muscle behind their spears, but they won't be a weak link that others have to protect. I think if we kept them behind it would do more harm to their spirits than anything. They want to be able to help their families and their town. I'd send them."

***

Amundr had walked over to the far corner of the courtyard where Herfinnr was instructing Saegrimr in proper sword fighting technique. "Move your feet! It's all about balance and mobility. With a spear there is much more weight in the weapon. The length and balance of a pole weapon force you to have a more rigid posture and be less mobile. Fighting with a sword you need to flow like water. Keep your shield up! You'd be better not carrying a shield than to carry it like that. At least it wouldn't be slowing you down." Amundr stood nearby and watched his friend get thrashed soundly for a few minutes while Herfinnr shouted admonitions that were variations on this same theme.

Finally, Saegrimr noticed that Amundr had returned. He paused and turned to speak to him. Herfinnr swept him off his feet with the wooden practice sword. "...and NEVER let your guard down in the middle of a fight!" he yelled. "Hello Amundr. Ready to get in some practice? I think Saegrimr is ready to take a break." From his position on the ground Saegrimr moaned feebly.

"Sure," Amundr said. "Where do I need to put this?" he asked, indicating the sword he had been given in the armory that morning. "The Duke says I am to have the sword I found."

"We'll take it to the armory later. For now you need to help your lazy friend up off his back and use his wooden sword. I don't think you'll be able to swing it hard enough to really hurt me and I'll pull my punches with you. We need to keep you in good enough shape to head out when the troops leave."

"The Duke says we're leaving in three days."

"Three days? That means we have plenty of time to practice and whip you two into shape." From the ground, Saegrimr moaned again.

Chapter Twelve

All that afternoon they practiced in the courtyard. The next day Herfinnr had them practicing all day. "We've got another sparring partner this morning," he said. "The Duke thought it would be best if he got some practice in as well since his sword technique could use some improvement." Amundr and Saegrimr looked up and saw that Aoalbert was walking sullenly behind Herfinnr.

"That's not all that could use improvement," Amundr muttered angrily.

"I think that I'll start off working with Saegrimr again and Amundr can work with Aoalbert." This elicited a groan from Saegrimr, but Amundr had a feral grin across his face as he rose to spar with Aoalbert.

Herfinnr handed each of them a wooden practice sword and made sure their armor and shields were positioned correctly. "Let's begin."

Amundr and Aoalbert circled each other while Herfinnr launched straight into another ferocious and direct assault on Saegrimr. Amundr was briefly distracted as his friend was knocked to the ground again and Aoalbert lunged quickly, striking him across his wrist and forcing him to drop his sword.

"Peasant," Aoalbert hissed as Amundr stooped to pick up his weapon. "You are adequate with a spear, but you'll never make a decent swordsman. You're just not of the right blood."

Something inside Amundr snapped. He waded in against Aoalbert, heedless of the blows glancing off his shield. He lashed out as hard as he could with his sword, striking the baron's son across the ribs once, twice, thrice. Aoalbert went down in a heap. Amundr was screaming incoherently about Aoalbert's cowardice and incompetence and as he went to strike the downed man he was seized firmly from behind by Herfinnr. "Save it for the vergrinn. We'll be seeing them soon enough. I think Aoalbert has learned enough for now." Aoalbert was dismissed to limp back into the keep, clutching his side tightly with his arm.

***

The following morning they moved their practices inside because of a constant drizzle. Late that afternoon, Herfinnr announced that their practice was complete. "For now, anyway," he had said. "We need to ensure that each of you have all of your gear and provisions prepared for the trip.

Thousands of men had come to the citadel from the surrounding area. Amundr and Saegrimr had been moved out of the barracks and into a small room in the keep "as befitted their station." They missed the boys from their town and they missed Stigr and Fastbjorn, who treated all the "lads" like their own sons. They went with Herfinnr to check on the last preparations of their horses and tack before heading with him to the great hall.

"It's a tradition that we have a feast before heading out," Herfinnr explained. "One great feast of rich meats and fresh baked goods to remind us of the homes and hearths we are setting out to protect. It also might be the last fresh food you eat for a while, so eat up." Amundr felt bad for his friends back in the barracks who usually ate much poorer fare until Herfinnr assured him "All the fighting men who are setting out partake in the feast. The whole courtyard will be full of men celebrating. They won't be up late – we're leaving at dawn – but they'll eat well."

The hall was filled with nobles. As the newest knights, Amundr and Saegrimr expected that they would be at the tables farthest from the dais, but they were actually seated at the table nearest the dais. "You are of the Order of the Rock – the Duke's own men," Herfinnr explained. "In the Duke's citadel, that outranks the knights of any other house save the king, and none of his men are here."

Indeed, Amundr noticed as he looked around the room that several of the other knights were looking at them and commenting on the sigils of rank they bore. As he looked around he realized that he did not see Aoalbert anywhere. When he brought this to Herfinnr's attention, Herfinnr scowled. "Of course not. This feast is for the men going out to battle, remember? The Duke has forbidden Aoalbert from riding with the company." Herfinnr did not approve of Aoalbert's cowardice, but he was in the service of Aoalbert's father. The baron would not be pleased with this turn of events.

After everyone had eaten their fill, the Duke stood up at the high table. "My faithful and courageous men," he began. "Tonight we celebrate life and home and hearth. Tonight we eat at peace and in comfort. Tomorrow we depart for battle." He paused before continuing. "We know not exactly how many vergrinn are menacing Eyjolf. Reports said at least two thousands, but more than five hundreds have already been slain. I had hoped to send three thousands to Eyjolf, but our muster has not been as quick as I had hoped. Tomorrow we will send two thousands of our foot men north with three hundred cavalry and two hundred mounted knights. We will end this invasion and we will end it quickly." He glanced at Amundr and Amundr feared the Duke would reveal what he knew of the Wolf Spears. "Get a good night's sleep and be ready to depart ere sunup."

***

An hour before sunrise Herfinnr came and roused Amundr and Saegrimr. "Cold biscuits and jerky this morning, boys. We need to get our horses ready so that we are ready to leave when the rest of the men are."

Amundr and Saegrimr had each packed their meager possessions in a small bag the previous evening, so they grabbed their bags and followed Herfinnr to the stable just off the courtyard. Their horses had been fed and were being saddled by stable boys. "Four score mounted spearmen and a score of mounted knights will be heading out ahead of us to scout," Herfinnr explained. "They will make sure the road is clear and identify places for us to camp each night. The foot men will follow at the best pace they can manage, and the rest of the horse will be following them."

It had taken six days to travel from Eyjolf to Gudmund, but Herfinnr told them that the men might make it in four if they pushed hard on the return trip. "We don't have women and children, and we're all men in good health or on horse. We're not as worried about being cautious. I'd wager the Duke will push hard for three or four days and then take it easy and arrive in five days ready for battle."

Their preparations complete, the three men led their horses out into the courtyard where many of the Duke's men were gathered. The Duke and his knights would lead a procession through the streets, picking up men as they passed barracks throughout the city. Once they exited the city gates, they would peel off into a field to set the order of march for their journey to Eyjolf.

At a signal from the Duke, the men in the courtyard all mounted their horses. He paused to speak to the men who were being left in charge of the defense of the city in his absence before swinging into his saddle. He turned towards the gate, drew his sword and shouted "To victory!" All the men in the courtyard drew their swords and shouted the same.

***

Amundr, Saegrimr, and Herfinnr found themselves in the last row of knights departing the courtyard. Women of all ages lined the streets along with children and elderly men, cheering them as they proceeded down the winding streets to the city gates. As they proceeded, Amundr noticed that men on foot and horseback joined their procession on several occasions.

As they passed through the city and to the gates, Amundr's spirits swelled with the cheering crowd. *This* was why he was here. *These* were the people his forefathers had sworn to protect with their very lives. This was his purpose.

He turned to look at Saegrimr on his left and noticed that his friend was similarly caught up in the moment. Just past Saegrimr, Herfinnr was grinning. "I see both of you have caught the alforn – the spirit of battle of the city of Gudmund. Try to remember that feeling after almost a week on the road when the spirit of battle will really matter."

They proceeded out of the city gates and the horsemen turned into an open field to the left of the road and dismounted. The scouting party was sent on ahead and the foot soldiers were organized into companies ranging in size from thirty to two hundreds. The foot soldiers began marching off down the road, and the last company was the batch of young recruits from Eyjolf. Finally, after the two thousand foot soldiers had begun their journey, the remainder of the cavalry mounted their horses and Amundr and Saegrimr were marching off to battle the vergrinn.

Chapter Thirteen

They rode in silence. At mid-morning, the cavalry came to the bridge over the Svanr River. Every man in the column had heard of what had transpired here the previous week. None said a word as Herfinnr, Amundr, and Saegrimr turned aside from the path and dismounted near the bridge.

The three knelt in silence, yet in their silence each was unique. Amundr lifted his eyes to the heavens and asked for the strength to carry on his father's legacy. Saegrimr lowered his face to the ground and begged for the wisdom necessary to guide him in these painful times. Herfinnr looked at them both, appreciative of the sacrifices that had been made here and wondering whether they could do what needed to be done in the days ahead. After several moments, they all stood and mounted their horses. They quickly caught up with the column of horsemen and fell in at the rear of the formation.

They rode on in silence for several more hours before pausing briefly to eat and feed the horses. Herfinnr explained that since they had scouts checking the road ahead and they were such a large force, they could press on after sunset as long as they could still see the road. They would continue to journey until they came to whatever place the scouts had decided they should rest. They would wake early and the scouts would take to the road by sunrise so that the army could march the entire day.

They proceeded thus day after day, until at the end of the fourth day of travel Amundr realized that they were approaching the very hill where they had spent their first night on their journey from Eyjolf to Gudmund. "Follow me," Herfinnr said, "The Duke has called for all the knights and the captains to meet atop the hill for a council of war. We should be at Eyjolf by tomorrow afternoon."

***

The knights and the captains milled around nervously at the top of the hill. Taken together there were over 250 of them, and they were waiting for the last of the scouts to report in. The knights were positioned in ranks around the outer edge of the hills, while the captains of the various companies of spearmen were nearest the fire. After what seemed like hours, the sound of hooves coming up the trail silenced the crowd. A hardened old man slipped from his steed and knelt before the Duke.

"Milord, we have scouted all the way to Eyjolf. The vergrinn are in the open plain before the town, but we only make their number to be eight hundreds." A murmur arose from the captains. Eight hundred vergrinn represented no mean opponent, but they had expected almost twice that number.

"And the town?"

"The town was dark, but we could spy men in the citadel, and figures moving upon the walls of the town itself."

"Then we are in time. I judge that the remainder must have left these to watch over the city while they sack the villages and homesteads of the surrounding countryside. We must dispatch these quickly so we may pursue the others." A cheer arose from the men atop the hill. "Our plan is simple. We will set out at first light. By mid day we will be within a league of the city. The infantry will march directly to the city walls and the cavalry will circle around the city and approach from the north. We will sweep down upon the beasts and skewer them between the horse and the foot. Hopefully the men of the city will see what is happening and send a sortie out as well. That should put the terror in those devils!"

The captains of the companies were each tasked with an approach to the city and the final preparations were made. Harnesses and weapons were checked and re-checked and the soldiers all received encouragement and instruction from their captains before settling down for the night. It was the third watch of the night when everything went wrong.

***

Amundr was sleeping fitfully. In his dreams the vergrinn were everywhere. They were snatching people from villages and slaying cattle for sport. He somehow knew that they were looking specifically for him, and they knew that the way to get him to come to them was to go after the people. He woke in a cold sweat. He half imagined he heard orders being given, and wondered if he wasn't still dreaming about the final instructions from the captains of the cavalry. He, Saegrimr, and Herfinnr were sleeping to the southeast of the base of the hill with the rest of the company from Eyjolf. As his mind cleared of sleep, he still heard the orders being whispered in the darkness in a low, guttural voice. "Longfang and Blackclaw have taken out the last sentries on this side of the hill. As soon as we hear back from Left Ear and Snarl we'll attack." Realization dawned on him – he was understanding something that was not human speech!

Amundr was on his feet in an instant, sword in hand and screaming at the top of his lungs. "Ambush! The sentries are dead and the vergrinn are upon us! Wake up! Ambush!"

C

A long howl arose in the woods and was answered by howls all around. The horses whinnied in terror and men all around were beginning to arise groggily from their beds. Amundr, sword drawn, charged towards the voices that had woken him.

***

The cry echoed up the hillside. "Awake! Awake! The enemy is upon us!" The men of the muster of Gudmund slowly rallied to the defense of the hill. At the top of the hill, the Duke ordered the fires to be fed and the standard to be raised as a rallying point. He looked around in vain for the young Spear Amundr. He was curious to see what he did in this fight.

In the dim light of the watch fires scattered around the hill the Duke could see shapes moving. Vergrinn were falling upon the various companies of men camped around the base of the hill, and the men were in chaos. The horses were pulling at their tethers and men were scrambling for weapons. As the Duke surveyed the hillside, he realized that the forces to the southeast seemed to be doing the best at holding their own, while those to the southwest were in trouble. He led his men in a charge down the hill to shore up the forces to the southwest.

***

The reason the forces to the southeast were holding their own was because they had the greatest warning. Amundr's cries had roused those around him and while he charged toward the enemy near him they were already rising and reaching for weapons.

Amundr's blade flashed a dull red in the darkness, and as he approached the vergrinn he saw their consternation. "You will pay tonight, beasts!" he said as he charged the nearest one. The consternation of the vergrinn turned to shock. They had understood him!

Frozen in shock, the first vergrinn fell headless at Amundr's first stroke. The second lost a forepaw and the knife it held. Oddly, none of the vergrinn he could see carried a spear. They all seemed to carry sharp flint knives. There had been four of them facing him, and the three still standing moved as if they were going to surround him.

When using a spear, the weapon's bulk would have made it difficult to use when defending against multiple foes at once. A well balanced sword in the hands of an agile young man was another story entirely. He remembered Herfinnr's instruction and allowed himself to flow from foe to foe, a macabre dance that saw vergrinn limbs severed and thrusts deep into his foes' torsos which drew howls of pain and rage. A second foe fell, missing his leg below the knee. The third, whose arm had been severed earlier now fell to a thrust through his throat. Amundr spun towards the last vergrinn, but was knocked aside by its paw. His sword spun out of his grasp and he looked up into its face, certain his doom had come. Suddenly from the darkness to his side two more large forms leapt towards him, growling in anger.

Chapter Fourteen

The two forms collided with the vergrinn menacing Amundr and bore it to the ground. In the dim light Amundr recognized his two dogs, Samr and Gramr! He looked around for his sword as he heard the dogs fighting the vergrinn. Desperately, he grabbed the blade from where it had fallen and rose to rejoin the fight.

Samr was flung through the air and landed at the base of a nearby tree, unmoving. Gramr had been shaken loose and he and the vergrinn were now warily eyeing each other.

"Gramr, heel!" Amundr said. Gramr hesitated, but withdrew behind his master. Amundr lunged towards the vergrinn, slicing deeply into his torso and removing his arm with his backstroke.

Gramr's whines drew Amundr's attention. He knelt beside Samr's still form and found that the hilt of the vergrinn's flint knife was sticking out of a gaping wound in his side. He stroked his faithful dog's muzzle and said "Oh, poor Samr. Brave, loyal Samr. I'm so sorry. Go in peace."

Amundr paused to catch his breath and survey his surroundings. The lads from Eyjolf were putting up a terrific fight back towards the hill and he could hear the sounds of the struggle all around him. He sprinted back towards his friends to help.

The advantage of surprise gone, the vergrinn still fought hard and wounded many men. A long howl rose from the woods to the east and from within every hunting pack of vergrinn engaged in combat, one of the beasts withdrew. They took advantage of the noise and confusion to slip silently away from their enemies, following the new Pack philosophy of retreating to bear news.

The last of the vergrinn still fighting were slain in short order, and the Duke called for the captains to take a census of their men and meet once again on top of the hill.

***

The captains reported in that the census was complete. They had lost eight score men to the surprise attacks, and most of the horses were now running free in the woods. The sentries who were on watch were mostly dead with the exception of a few on the west wide of the hill.

"...overall, we did well considering what happened to the sentries. It was a good thing someone stumbled upon the vergrinn when they did." The Duke's war leader finished his report and stepped back.

"Thank you. At least now we know where the vergrinn went who were missing from Eyjolf. I want our men to tally the corpses and determine how many of the foul creatures were slain." The Duke paused. "Haul the vergrinn carcasses to the clearing on the east side of the road and burn them. We need to rest for a few more hours before moving on."

As the captains broke up, the Duke turned to his war leader. "Things could have gone much worse. Who raised the alarm?"

"I don't know for certain. Most of the men think it came from one of the kids down there." He gestured towards the encampment of the men from Eyjolf. The Duke raised his eyebrows. Perhaps there was something to the legend of the Wolf Spears after all.

***

The next morning, the camp was abuzz. They had sent out parties of trackers to find the horses, and of the five hundred horse they had started with, one hundred were missing or dead. Of the dead men, two score had been cavalry, so three score of the mounted spearmen were forced to march in the companies of foot soldiers.

It turned out that they had killed three hundred vergrinn the night before. That still meant that with the five hundred previously slain and the eight hundred on the plains before the town, there were four hundred vergrinn unaccounted for if the earlier count of two thousand was correct.

"I don't like this," the Duke said to his war leader. "They must have seen our scouts and followed them back to our camp. Instead of attacking, they waited and brought reinforcements. That's just not something the vergrinn do. Men everywhere reported that vergrinn retreated last night during the battle, so their main force must know we are coming now. I hope the missing four hundreds don't have any more surprises in store for us."

It was mid-morning before they set out for Eyjolf. They were four leagues from the city walls and a hard march would take three hours. They took an easier pace to conserve their strength for the coming battle, so it was that in mid-afternoon as the late autumn sun was already sinking low they came at last to the relief of Eyjolf.

***

When Eyjolf had been built after the last vergrinn war, the forest had been clear cut in a circle three miles across. The location had been chosen for the springs of water that were located at the center of the circle, and the town was located in the center of the circle over the springs. The keep was located in the center of the town and the springs were within its walls. The walls of the city were fifteen feet high and constructed from logs as thick as a man's forearm was long, while the keep was mostly of stone with walls thirty feet high and taller than any nearby building.

The King of Alarr and the Duke of Gudmund had used the lumber from the forest in the construction of the town walls and several common buildings. The lumber that remained was made available to settlers to help them construct their homes and barns, and rock had been quarried from outcroppings near Eagle Point. Saegrimr's village was actually founded by folk working in the quarry or supplying the workers with food and trade goods.

As Amundr, Saegrimr, and the rest of the mounted men circled the city at the edge of the woods, the youngest knights began to wonder what lay ahead. Neither of them had ever fought in mounted combat such as this, and Herfinnr had mostly schooled them in fighting with sword and shield in a standing position. They were both fair horsemen, but neither was practiced in firing a bow from a saddle or in using his spear as a lance. At the edge of the clearing, Amundr had ordered Gramr to stay. He would return for him when time allowed, but the dog would likely just be in the way on the battlefield.

Amundr looked back and saw that the infantry were almost to the city walls away to the south of the city. He wondered what kind of reception they would get from the people of Eyjolf.

***

The footmen of the muster of Gudmund were marching steadily towards the city of Eyjolf. In the distance, they could see men atop the battlements of the keep, waving excited greetings to them. The defenders were shouting and pointing towards the vergrinn in the distance, but over the din of the marching men nothing could be heard at this distance. They marched steadily onward. The vergrinn in the open plain before them made no move to retreat, apparently realizing that there was nowhere to flee to on the open plain. They had shifted position slightly, and it was disappointing to see that unless they were driven back considerably by the cavalry's initial charge, any sortie mounted by the city's defenders through the main gate would come from behind the advancing infantry instead of from the vergrinn's flanks.

The cavalry had finally moved into position and the Duke slowly led them towards the vergrinn. Their plan was to approach within bowshot and begin shooting vergrinn at range. The vergrinn would either charge the cavalry or, more likely in the Duke's estimation, flee before them in a panic.

As the cavalry approached, the vergrinn remained in position. A long howl rose over the plain, which Amundr understood to mean "Be steady. Wait for our moment." As he puzzled over this, he saw that the vergrinn were propping up large rectangular wooden shapes and were ducking behind them. They were using shields! The cavalry approached to within 150 yards before beginning to fire an ineffective volley of arrows towards the vergrinn. Something about the shields they were using struck him as odd, but he couldn't quite figure out what it was.

**

The infantry were approaching from the rear, and they saw that the vergrinn were raising shields to protect against a volley of arrows from the cavalry. Several of the captains smiled. They would get to draw first blood. "String your bows and prepare to fire! We'll close to within bowshot and we'll have them from both directions!" The cry went up and down the line to ready bows.

In the distance, the Duke saw the infantry approach to within two hundred yards and lay down their spears and shields to ready their bows. This wasn't exactly how he had envisioned the battle, but it would be effective nonetheless. In the distance he saw the gates to the city opening and he hoped the city's defenders wouldn't draw the attention of the vergrinn to the bowmen behind them.

***

Suddenly, Amundr realized what bothered him about the shields. They were doors! The vergrinn must have dragged every door from every dwelling for miles around, but even that wouldn't have been enough. Where could the doors have come from? He looked in the distance behind the infantry and saw the city gate a quarter mile away. It had opened, and he could barely make out a few dark figures moving around near it. They were sneaking out and then disappearing in the tall grass of the plain between the city and the approaching infantry whose back was turned to the gate.

"It's a trap! The vergrinn have taken the city and are sneaking up on our men from behind!" Amundr rode over to the Duke and repeated his warning. The Duke looked out across the field and quickly came to a decision. He seized a horn and sounded the charge. Horsemen all across the line spurred their horses forward as fast as they would go.

Across the field, the infantry wondered what was happening. "We can't fire at them now! What is the Duke thinking?" All down the lines the captains told their men to ready their spears and shields and prepare to meet the vergrinn in melee combat.

***

The vergrinn knew their plan had gone awry, but they still thought they might catch the foot soldiers unaware. They turned towards the approaching infantry and ran at them as fast as they could, snarling and growling. Their noise masked the noise of their brethren approaching from the rear and prevented the humans from hearing the warnings being shouted by the approaching cavalry.

The infantry braced themselves and set their spears to absorb the charge of the rapidly approaching vergrinn line. There were more than two men for each of the approaching vergrinn, so they felt confident of their ability to handle the enemy.

Across the field, the cavalry urged as much speed as they could from their horses. Amundr, Saegrimr, and a few other men who were smaller of stature and lighter, outpaced the rest. In a few seconds they were streaking past the vergrinn and Amundr was screaming "Behind you! They're coming up behind you!"

Some of the infantry heard the screams and turned back towards the town. "We're surrounded!" A few of the captains kept their heads and ordered some of their men to face each threat, but several companies were thrown into confusion and the company on the eastern flank of the formation panicked and fled towards the tree line.

The leading edge of the cavalry reached the vergrinn just before they met the infantry. They struck and swept past, veering sharply to avoid the spears of their comrades at arms. They picked their way past the infantry and sought the vergrinn who had been sneaking up behind them. The vergrinn had long spears and strong arms, and they had learned the art of setting their spears to check a cavalry charge. For the moment, both sides paused to re-evaluate the situation.

The cavalry had finished their initial sweep through the vergrinn line and had felled a quarter of the enemy with minimal losses. The infantry now re-formed their ranks while the cavalry swept behind them to deal with the vergrinn ambushers. No longer concerned with the threat to their rear, the infantry advanced. With the vergrinn losses, there were now almost three men in the infantry line for every vergrinn they faced. The two lines met, and the overwhelming numerical superiority quickly turned the battle into a rout.

Meanwhile, the full cavalry force was now circling between the former vergrinn ambushers and the infantry formation. Neither side was willing to close the distance – the cavalry's primary advantage of speed and mobility thwarted by the vergrinn formation being arrayed like a company of pikemen.

"Ready bows," the Duke ordered. The vergrinn saw the horsemen readying their bows and decided the time had come to charge. The mounted men loosed a volley of arrows that dropped a hundred vergrinn in their tracks before they had to set aside their bows and take up their swords and spears.

Unwilling to let the vergrinn attack the rear of the infantry formation, the Duke and his men held their ground. The numbers were much more even in this skirmish than in any of their previous encounters, and the vergrinn's superior strength was taking a toll. More experienced knights fought as one with their mounts, the horses kicking at any enemy within reach. Inexperienced horse warriors such as Amundr either clung to their mounts as they attempted to flee in terror or were flung from their backs. Amundr managed to skewer a vergrinn on his spear, but his horse reared and the spear was wrenched from his grasp.

Amundr drew his sword to go after the next vergrinn. The red blade caught the light of the afternoon sun and suddenly looked as if it was a flaming brand, burning brightly to hold back the tide of darkness. The reaction was instantaneous. Every vergrinn on the field raised their voice in an eerie, pained howl. There was an answering howl from the edge of the forest, but the men from Gudmund took advantage of the temporary distraction to strike decisively at their foes. In a few moments, the battle was over.

Chapter Fifteen

The men of the muster of Gudmund had lost two hundreds in this battle. The vergrinn had lost twelve hundreds. The total number of vergrinn dead in the two weeks since the invasion had started was two thousands, while the duchy of Gudmund had lost fewer than four hundreds. By any measure, the men of Gudmund had won a decisive victory, yet to them it felt otherwise.

The baron and his men had met the Duke at the gates of the city at the conclusion of the battle. The baron guided them down the narrow streets of Eyjolf toward the keep. As he turned to speak with the Duke, he glanced around, looking for Aoalbert. "Is Aoalbert with you?" he asked.

The Duke and Herfinnr exchanged a dark glance. The baron did not fail to notice this. "Is he...dead?" The baron appeared stricken.

"He lives, milord," Herfinnr offered. "He remained at the citadel. It would be best if we discussed him later."

The baron looked around at the small company of men and said "Yes, of course. Your men must be exhausted. We did not hope to have relief for several days yet. We have food and fire. I would not enter any of the buildings out in the town alone until we can ensure no vergrinn remained behind."

"Thank you. We would appreciate it," said the Duke. "Perhaps you and I can withdraw to your study and discuss a few matters after we see to the men."

"Of course," the baron called for several men and began issuing commands regarding the preparation of food and arrangements for lodging. As there was insufficient room in the keep, the men would be camping on the open plain before Eyjolf, but they would have large watch fires and doubled sentries.

***

Before the baron and the Duke withdrew to converse, the Duke held a council of war in the baron's hall. He called upon the baron. "Before we do anything else, let's hear the full tale of the siege of Eyjolf."

The baron grimaced. "They took the city a few days after we sent our women and children away," he said. "We withdrew to the keep and were hard pressed to hold them out. If the women and children had still been here there would not have been room for all." He took a deep breath before continuing. "They came in the still of a foggy night bearing ladders and scaled the wall. We lost many men holding them back, and we feared we would not hold the keep. Yesterday after sunset a large force of them withdrew from the town and headed south down the road and we hoped that meant you were on your way. If they had kept up their determined assault, I don't know how much longer we could have held out, even in the keep." He gathered his thoughts. "The vergrinn are smart. All the old tales described them as vicious brutes. These beasts had the cunning of the best hunters. They lulled us into complacency and struck only at the most opportune times." With sadness in his voice, he finished, "If they return in numbers, we cannot hold the city. The keep is too small to house the defenders."

The Duke said nothing for several minutes. Finally he spoke. "We must send scouts to track these beasts back to their homes. We must find their dens and destroy them utterly. We will do this in the morning." With that he dismissed the men and withdrew with the baron for a private conversation.

***

"It is as I feared," said the baron. "I believed Aoalbert was not up to the responsibilities and I hoped beyond hope that such a journey would help him find his way. I regret the loss of my men on that journey, but the story of their heroism will lift the spirits of my people for years to come. Eight stood against five hundred? Truly?"

The Duke nodded. "Your men have fought and died well. The youngest no less well than the eldest. You did well sending the younglings along as part of the muster to protect the women and children. If folk in all towns raised their young like the people of Eyjolf raise theirs, the kingdom would stand forever."

"Like all people of Eyjolf save the baron himself," the baron said, rebuking himself harshly.

"You have done well in all matters surrounding these difficult times. I will not judge you based on the actions of your son any more than I would judge him based on your choices and actions. The child will not share the guilt of the parent, nor will the parent share the guilt of the child." He paused. "I will speak to you of the other young men. Amundr, Saegrimr, and the rest. As you know, I have knighted Amundr and Saegrimr. They are of the Order of the Rock, and their duty is now to myself and my lands. Until the vergrinn are defeated, I would take the rest of the men you sent to Gudmund as your contribution to my muster. You may keep every man who remained in Eyjolf for the siege, but Stigr, Fastbjorn, and even Herfinnr will be mine along with all the young men."

"All the young men?" The Duke nodded. "Even Aoalbert?"

The Duke nodded yet again. "I think Aoalbert needs to learn the lessons we learned as lads – that the responsibility of the nobles is to serve the people, not be served by them. To that end I will be stripping him of his knighthood and assigning him to serve one of my knights as a squire, until such time as he has proven his worth and may reclaim his title and his station as your heir."

The baron was horrified. His only son was being removed from his station. He stared at the Duke in silence as he mulled this over for several long moments. "You think he will learn humility?"

"He will."

"You will keep him safe?"

"As safe as any squire may be during time of war."

The baron was silent for another moment before he found his voice. "It would be good for Aoalbert to learn humility and the meaning of sacrifice. Which knight is he going to serve?"

***

The next morning the Duke sent three parties of scouts out to hunt down the vergrinn that had escaped. He gave explicit instructions to them to track them back to their dens and report back on their locations. The men were selected from among the best trackers and woodsmen and were sent on their way by mid-morning.

Other, larger groups were sent to evaluate the condition of nearby villages and round up the livestock that had fled in terror from the vergrinn. The rest of the people thoroughly searched the town of Eyjolf by daylight to ensure that no vergrinn had remained behind before assembling in and around the church to give thanks for their salvation. That evening, after the first groups sent to search the area returned, the Duke proclaimed that there would be a celebratory feast the next night. Much of the livestock had survived and while many homes were destroyed, few people had been lost.

The celebratory feast was enjoyed by all. Amundr and Saegrimr found themselves in the unaccustomed position of being the center of attention for many young ladies around their age. Saegrimr danced and talked and laughed with many of the girls, but Amundr sat quietly nearby.

Finally Saegrimr came over and spoke to him. "Little Mundi, enjoy yourself! We have not only saved our people, we have won honor and glory and have joined the ranks of the nobility. If there was ever a night to celebrate, it is tonight!"

Amundr looked at Saegrimr, about to speak, then closed his mouth. He looked down, then looked out at the crowd of people enjoying themselves, then looked back at his best friend. "You're right. This is what we fought for. This is what the others died for. We're here so that they may have life, and have it more abundantly!" Amundr got up, accepted an invitation to dance, and celebrated joyously for the rest of the evening.

***

In three days time the first of the scouts reported back. They immediately went to consult the baron and the Duke. Their faces looked grim and their horses were almost dead from exhaustion.

The baron and the Duke were waiting for the scouts in the great hall of the keep. The baron was slightly dismayed by the similarity between this meeting and one held a few weeks before. The scouts came in and bowed to the Duke and then to the baron.

"Were you able to track the vergrinn?" the Duke asked.

"We were," Stigr said.

"Did they return to their dens?"

"No milord. We tracked them until they met up with another force of their kind coming from the mountains to the north."

The Duke and the baron looked at each other. "Another force? Heading this way?"

"Yes milord. I anticipate they will be here in three days. The remainder of the scouts are positioned at various points between here and there to gather more information and report back."

"How many were there?"

Stigr hesitated. "Milord, we were not in a position to be able to see their entire force. What we did see numbered over ten thousands." The Duke sank back into his seat. Ten thousand vergrinn. The force they had faced previously had been but the vanguard of this larger force. Ten thousands was almost twice as large as the force he brought with to Eyjolf and the force he had left to guard Gudmund combined. Eyjolf was lost, and Gudmund might very well be also.

"Summon the people. We are withdrawing to Gudmund. No one is to remain behind."

The rest of the day was spent planning and organizing the withdrawal. Every cart and wagon was laden with goods and with people who were unable to walk long distances. The Duke and the baron divided these into four groups and assigned just under a quarter of the men at arms to journey with each group. The Duke was tasked with leading the first group and the baron was entrusted to lead the last group, which would include the livestock. Amundr and Saegrimr were assigned to the first group of men who were returning to Gudmund with the Duke. Saegrimr's father Holmr was sent with this group so that he could spend some time with his son. A hundred men were left at the keep to await the return of the scouts. They were given explicit instructions to leave no later than the morning Stigr had said the vergrinn might arrive. The scouts returned, were met by their comrades, and departed for Gudmund.

Eyjolf was abandoned to the enemy.

Epilogue

As the moon rose over the horizon, Whitefoot looked out over the clench. Thousands of members of the Pack had died since the last clench, but the price had been worth it. They had taken the first steps towards cleansing the land and destroying their enemies. The place where they were assembling was the location of the Great Cull, the Pack's greatest defeat. Now, it was the focal point of their victory celebration.

He had much to think on. They had caused the enemy to flee before them and several of their new tactics had been successful, yet he was bothered. Surviving members of the First Claw had reported that the enemy had possessed the Bloodfang, an ancient weapon the rumor of which had been passed down through the generations. If the Bloodfang was here, the Destroyers might be here as well. The Pack had thought they wiped out the Destroyers thousands of moons ago, and the stories said the Bloodfang had disappeared at the same time as the Destroyers. He would have all of his scouts watch and listen for any hint of either, but tonight they would celebrate.

The moon approached its zenith while Whitefoot watched over the clench. His people had feasted sumptuously over the past few days and were contented. "My children," he began, "We have lost much, but we have gained much more. Eat, sleep, celebrate. Tomorrow we will begin taking steps that will allow us to rid ourselves of these humans forever!"

The howls of the Pack lasted long into the night.

***

Six days after they departed Eyjolf, the Duke and the first exhausted group of refugees finally reached the city. Saegrimr's mother Hafbera and his younger sisters and brothers had been sent to Gudmund with the original convoy weeks before. During that first trip to Gudmund, he and Amundr had been unable to spend much time with them because they were hurried into training to prepare for the return to Eyjolf.

Hafbera embraced her husband and her son warmly, then turned to Amundr. "We heard about your father. We are so sorry. From this day you will always be a son to us." Amundr looked up at her, then at Holmr, who smiled and nodded. They were offering to formally adopt him into their family so that he would have legal standing and protection. It was a kind gesture.

"Thank you both. You will always be closer to me than anyone else still living, but now Saegrimr and I are men. We are in the Duke's service." Saegrimr's parents had noticed their armor and swords, but had said nothing.

Saegrimr was being swarmed by his younger brothers and sisters, all eager to know about his adventures. He told them the story of their journeys, and was hit with a hundred questions.

"Did you really fight ten thousand vergrinn?"

"Were you scared?"

"Can I have a sword too?"

"What was the ocean like?"

"Did you kill any vergrinn?"

"Are the vergrinn really living in our village now?"

"One at a time. One at a time. Yes, I did fight, and yes, it was scary, and yes, I killed vergrinn. I didn't kill nearly as many as Mundi, though." He looked over at his best friend and grinned. "Maybe he could tell you about fighting them alone and outnumbered in the dark in the middle of the forest in the dead of night."

His younger brothers wanted to hear that, but Hafbera interrupted. "I think the kids have heard enough about your adventures for now. Maybe later Amundr can tell them his story." She shot Saegrimr a stern look. His youngest brother and sister hadn't seen six winters and would be terrified by such tales. Amundr and Saegrimr spent the next several hours enjoying the company of Saegrimr's family.

***

"Your lordship, I have news." The arrival of the lore master stirred the Duke from his thoughts. "We have found another scroll in the archives. It was mislaid among various poems and other ancient trifles, but it is undoubtedly related to the matter at hand." The lore master raised a scroll tube. Unmistakable on its surface was the same unknown rune that had been present on the scroll tube that Amundr had found. "The contents are...fascinating."

He handed the scroll tube to the Duke. He opened it and took out the scroll. He read the scroll, then re-read it. Finally he spoke. "Have you told anyone else of this?" The lore master shook his head. "See that it stays that way.

***

Late in the night, the Duke sat alone deep in thought. The implications of what he had read were staggering indeed. He would send a messenger to

the King for advice at first light. He picked up the
scroll and re-read it one more time:

Though vergrinn are quite violent
The war can still be won
The vergrinn shall fall silent
When the Wolf Spears' task is done

When the last of the Spears has risen
Great victory shall he bring
Salvation shall be given
By the blood of the ancient King

The sword shall find its rightful hand
The throne its rightful heir
Blood shall flow throughout the land
And cries shall fill the air

The Spear shall know betrayal
By a hand that he did trust
His courage cannot fail
Before the final thrust

Not all life is victory
Not all death is loss
To make his final journey
The ocean he shall cross

Appendices

Pronunciation Guide

Name	Pronunciation
Adiarfr	EY-dee-AHRF
Alarr	EY-lahr
Aleifr	EY-leef
Alforn	EYL-fawrn
Amundr	AH-muhnd
Aoalbert	AL-bert
Eyjolf	AHY-johlf
Fastbjorn	FAST-byurn
Gedda	GED-ah
Gramr	GRAM
Gudmund	GOOD-muhnd
Hafbera	HAF-bair-AH
Hallr	HAWL
Herfinnr	HAIR-fin
Holmr	HOHM
Hundolfr	HUHN-dohlf
Igull	IG-ool
Mundi	MUHN-dee
Olafr	OO-lahf
Saegrimr	SOU-grim
Samr	SAM
Sjaundi	SYAWN-dee
Stigr	STIG
Svanr	SVAHN
Ulfbane	OOLF-beyn
Vergrinn	VER-grin

Dramatis Personae

Adiarfr	Grizzled trainer at Gudmund
Aleifr	Long dead Wolf Spear who hid the sword
Amundr	Young man from the woods near Eyjolf
Aoalbert	Son of the baron of Eyjolf
Fastbjorn	Merchant from Eyjolf
Gedda	Elder from a fishing village on the coast
Gramr	Amundr's black and grey Elkhound
Hafbera	Saegrimr's mother
Hallr	Man of the muster of Eyjolf
Herfinnr	Knight in the service of Eyjolf
Holmr	Saegrimr's father and a village elder
Hundolfr	Knight in the service of Eyjolf
Igull	Guard at the harbor of Gudmund
Olafr	Amundr's father
Saegrimr	Amundr's best friend
Samr	Amundr's jet black Elkhound
Stigr	The baron of Eyjolf's chief huntsman
Ulfbane	Long dead Duke of Gudmund
Vergrinn	Evil upright wolves
Whitefoot	Leader of the vergrinn

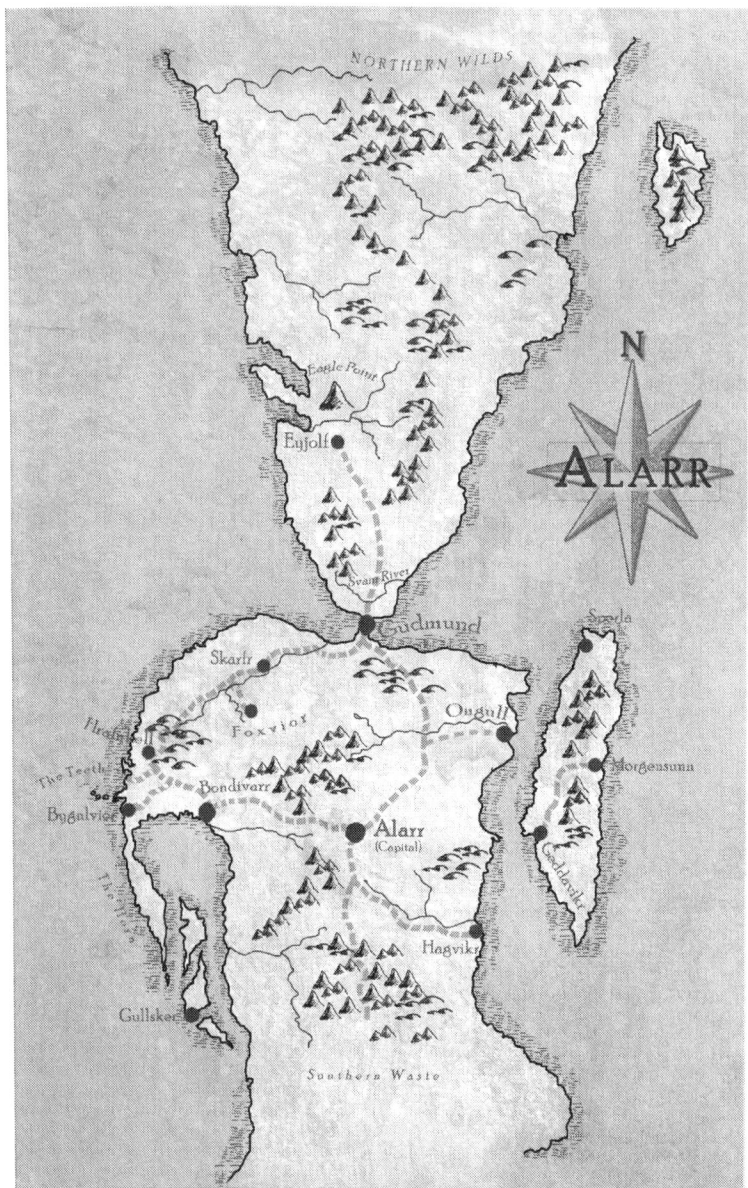

NORTHERN WILDS

Eagle Point

Eyjolf

Svan River

Gudmund

Skarlr

Ongull

Spola

Foxvjox

Hrafnfell

The Teeth

Bondivarr

Alarr
(Capital)

Morgensunn

Sea

Bygalvice

Gandavik

The Pillar

Hagvikr

Gullsker

Southern Waste

N

ALARR

Made in the USA
Charleston, SC
01 December 2014